adore me

THE
keatyn
CHRONICLES
adore me

JILLIAN DODD

Published by Swoonworthy Books, an imprint of Jillian Dodd, Inc.
www.jilliandodd.net

The Keatyn Chronicles and Jillian Dodd are registered trademarks of
Jillian Dodd, Inc.

Editor: Jovana Shirley, Unforeseen Editing
Photo: ©Regina Wamba
Cover Design: Mae I Designs

ISBN: 978-1-953071-13-2

This book is for

Melissa and Mireya,
the original KC Addicts.

Books by Jillian Dodd

London Prep
The Exchange
The Boys' Club
The Kiss
The Key

The Keatyn Chronicles®
Stalk Me
Kiss Me
Date Me
Love Me
Adore Me
Hate Me
Get Me
Fame
Power
Money
Sex
Love
Keatyn Unscripted
Aiden

That Boy
That Boy
That Wedding
That Baby
That Love
That Ring
That Summer
That Promise

Wednesday, November 23rd
RUINED MY LIPS.
12:30PM

I RE-READ THE moon in my hand.

While others may wish on a shooting star, it's the moon that holds my dreams afar.

I clutch it to my chest and take a deep breath while trying to figure out why Aiden would've written that.

I grab my phone, look up the quote on the internet, and get no hits.

Did he make it up?

My mind wanders to my own wish in the moonlight.

I shake my head. It can't be.

And if Aiden really did make a wish on the moon then it's official.

Fate is a cold-hearted bitch just like Aphrodite.

If Aiden truly was my fate, then fate would've allowed us to meet later in life.

Under different circumstances.

When I had gotten my life back, or when I had finally accepted that I'd never get it back.

A morbid thought flits through my brain. That I might not be here later in life.

A big part of me wants to turn the car around and go back to Eastbrooke.

I look at my phone and consider calling him. Consider reading all of his texts. Listening to all of his voicemails.

Asking him why he wrote on the moon.

But I can't.

I have to deal with Vincent first. I have to get my life back. And after that, I promised to give B a chance.

I need to forget about Aiden. Put Eastbrooke and the friends I made there behind me.

My leaving is for the best. For everyone's best.

I'm just not sure what's best for me.

I've been mulling over a lot of options. I've considered moving to my loft, getting my GED, and starting NYU in the fall. But that would mean hanging out with Jake and Dawson. It would mean coming in contact with new people. People who I couldn't make friends with.

I quickly ruled out that option.

Besides, I'm not going back to my loft.

I can't.

I'm pretty sure Aiden ruined it, just like he ruined my lips. I'll put it on the market and forget about it too.

I run my hand over my new four-leaf clover necklace and say a little prayer.

MY PHONE RINGS, so I stop praying and answer with a polite hello.

"Miss Monroe, this is Edward at Jet Co-op. Before you board, don't forget to stop in the office and sign the new paperwork."

"I won't," I say. But, obviously, I had forgotten.

I hang up and ask the driver to run me back to the office.

I get out of the car and pull my sunglasses over my eyes, partially to block the light and partially because I'm a little freaked out to even go inside. I'm worried Vincent sent my photo to every airport in America.

I put myself into my role. I'm not Keatyn Douglas who's being stalked. I'm Keatyn Monroe who's just an Eastbrooke student.

Was an Eastbrooke student, I think, suddenly fighting back tears.

I'm looking at the office building, but in my mind I'm seeing the beauty that is Eastbrooke. The gorgeous trees. The old brick buildings. The commons. The people. I'm really going to miss everyone. I hate that I didn't give them proper goodbyes. I hate that I did that to them. And most of all, I hate that I'm reliving this moment again.

I was stupid to go to Eastbrooke. Anyone in their right mind should've seen the potential problems.

But we weren't really in our right minds when we made the decision. We were scared.

And I'm done being that way.

It's time to take control of my life.

It's time to fight back.

I take a deep breath and breeze into the office like I don't have a care in the world.

"I'm Keatyn Monroe." I shake Edward's hand and then review the contract for the many additional hours that I purchased on a whim a couple of days ago. That was when one of my options included me turning the tables on Vincent and stalking him.

I decided that might not be my smartest idea ever.

Besides, a new plan is starting to take root. Cooper and

me on a farm in Iowa, way out in the country. Lots of acres where we can set up a firing range. A barn we can turn into a training facility. Maybe a few chickens, a cow, and a vegetable garden so that we would never have to leave. We could grow everything we eat.

Okay, maybe not. I don't think I could kill a chicken.

Or a carrot.

I think I'd prefer to buy my food already dead.

I've thought about marrying Cooper. Going Amish.

Living out my life in hiding.

I'm also strongly considering faking my own death.

I'd hate to do that to my family but if I did, I could kill Vincent. My family wouldn't have me, but they'd have their lives back. I could watch the girls grow up from afar.

Then, maybe I could become the CIA's youngest operative. Cooper and I could travel the world and spy.

I bet he'd look damn hot in a tuxedo.

Oooh, I know. I'm going to watch *Triple X* on the plane.

Oh, the things I'm gonna to do for my country.

While Edward goes in the back to make a copy for my records, I hear two ladies at the next counter gossiping about who's going to star in the next best-selling book turned movie.

One of them holds out a magazine. "Here, you can read this on your lunch break. Did you see the cover? I can't believe how scary skinny Abby Johnston has gotten. People think it's the stress of Tommy's affair."

"I wouldn't care what Tommy did as long as I could get a piece of that fine man. I'm not greedy. I'd be more than willing to share," she says with a chuckle.

"You're bad."

"But honest," she says as she wanders off with her lunch

bag. "Besides, I read that this morning."

I wander over and help myself to a bottle of water from the self-service bar, glancing at the photo on the magazine.

I think back to Vancouver. I noticed Mom looked thin, but she looks even skinnier now.

I get my paperwork back from Edward, step outside, and call Tommy.

I'll use this situation to set the first part of my plan in motion.

"I saw that magazine cover of Mom. She looks even thinner than she did at Gracie's birthday party. I'm worried about her, Tommy."

"I'm worried about her too," Tommy replies. "This thing. The guilt. The fear. The lying. It's eating her alive."

"You're almost done filming in Vancouver, right?"

"Yeah, we wrap up this week and then I'm scheduled to start *Trinity 3: Retribution* in New York with Matt."

"And she's supposed to start her publicity tour for *To Maddie, with Love*, right?"

"Yeah. That's why she hasn't been eating or sleeping. She's so afraid that all the press and promotion will really send Vincent over the edge."

"Cancel the tour. Break her contract. Pay them whatever you have to, Tommy. Get her out of it."

"I've considered that."

"You have to do more than consider it. You have to convince her. And I know you two don't like to be apart, but you shouldn't bring her and the girls to New York. Send them to France with James and don't tell anyone. Lie. Say she's sick. Say she's in rehab. Hire a battalion to guard the grounds if you have to, but I know she'll feel safe there."

"She's supposed to start another movie soon."

"Get her out of that too. I'm going to start putting

pressure on Vincent, and I need her and the girls somewhere safe."

"What kind of pressure?"

"Financial pressure. I mean, I won't be doing it personally, but, um, someone with like financial expertise will be. And that, combined with the timing of Mom's release—well, we just don't know how he'll react. That's why I really need them somewhere safe. Tommy, do you remember last spring when you asked me about a role in *Retribution*?"

"Of course. I was a little crushed when you told me you weren't interested."

"I was afraid I'd embarrass you. Will you tell me about the role?"

"An old enemy has you kidnapped and I go badass to save you. I want my last Trinity movie to be my best, and I just thought if you played my daughter, it would bring my feelings out more."

"I love you, Tommy. I don't tell you that enough, but I couldn't ask for a better dad."

"You mean stepdad?"

"No, I mean dad. And I know my real dad would be okay with me saying that."

"That means a lot to me. I'm sorry how things went down at the house. The girls were so happy to see you."

"I shouldn't have surprised you like that. And, don't worry; I won't be seeing them again. Not until this is over. So, would I need to audition for the role?"

"Hypothetically speaking?"

"Yes."

"You'd have to audition, but only as a formality. I had it all planned out so that you could shoot it over your Christmas break."

I don't bother telling him I'm not going back to school.

Or that the timing is perfect, because I'll be needing the spotlight about then.

"I want to do it."

"I wish you could."

"I'm working with Cooper on all of this. He says I can do it, and that he'll make sure I stay safe," I lie. Then I add sincerely, "It'd mean a lot to me, Tommy."

"That would be amazing."

"So you get Mom to France, and I'll do the movie. Deal?"

"Baby, you've got a deal."

WASH AWAY THE HURT.
1PM

AS I GET back into the car, I get a text.

> **Grandma:** *You've been asking a lot of questions about love and fate. Here's what I believe. Fate brings people into your life, but it's up to you to decide who gets to stay.*

I shove my phone into my bag, wishing it were that easy, and head toward the plane feeling sad.

I'll be fine once I get to the island. I'll build sandcastles, watch the water wash them away, and know I made the right decision about both Aiden and Eastbrooke.

I'm hoping the water will wash away some of the hurt, too. So that all I'm left with is anger. Anger that I'll direct towards Vincent until I destroy his life.

I take a step onto the plane, expecting to be greeted by my flight attendant.

Instead, I see Aiden and Peyton.

WTF!?

Doesn't that boy ever freaking listen to me?

I stand in the doorway, arms crossed in front of me, shaking my head.

Because, no.

No. No. No. No. No. No. No.

As if it isn't bad enough that Aiden is on my plane, he's fist-bumping the pilots like he owns the place.

I study him closely. His bruises are almost gone. His hair is perfectly messy. His shoulders are back and confident.

He looks more like his old self.

Damn him.

But I guess it's better than how he looked in the chapel and at the pep rally.

I close my eyes tightly, trying to forget, but knowing that in a few moments I'm going to make him look that way again.

Peyton sees me first, gives me an awkward smile, and brushes Aiden's arm to get his attention.

He freezes while the pilots and attendant introduce themselves and then get to work.

Then he uses those damn tractor beams to hold my gaze as he walks across the plane. I couldn't look away if I wanted to.

He grabs the crook of my elbow, causing me to jump, as he leads me to the back of the plane.

I'm pretty sure his touch was like a defibrillator, sending 360 joules of electricity straight to my heart.

Making it beat for him again.

Damn my traitorous heart.

Be strong, Keatyn. It doesn't matter what your heart feels.

You have to use your head.

He thinks this is the big gesture.

And it is.

It so is.

I so want to jump into his arms.

Tell him I'm sorry.

Kiss every inch of his face.

But I can't.

I squirm out of his hold but still end up trapped against the back wall. His tall, muscular chest is totally invading my personal space just like it did the first time I met him.

"You know you can't come with me."

He doesn't respond.

Well, he does respond, but his response is to grab both my arms and pull me into a kiss.

A hard, possessive kiss.

A cotton-candy-has-filled-my-brain kiss.

I do everything in my power to remain stiff.

But I can't.

Probably because of his godly love potion trickery.

And why the hell does he have to smell so good?

He pulls away, so I shake my head and start to speak.

But he stops me again with his lips.

After giving me another long kiss, he backs away slightly and cocks an eyebrow at me.

"You know you can't—" I try to say.

Kiss.

"Stop th—"

Another kiss.

"I'm going to keep kissing you until you stop talking," he tells me.

"But I—"

Kiss.

Ohmigawd, he is so frustrating.

"Aiden, but we already—"

His lips land hard on mine. Again.

And with every kiss, my resolve is weakening.

He stops kissing me and looks into my eyes.

I bite my lower lip to keep from saying anything else, while shaking my head, closing my eyes, and wishing I could close my ears.

Because I don't want to hear what he has to say.

It was hard enough to hear it once. To end it once.

His face is way too close to mine. I can feel the stubble on his cheek. His breath on my neck.

His finger touching my lip.

"Does this mean you're ready to listen?"

I shake my head no.

Because I can't listen. I can't hear it. It's why I couldn't listen to his messages or read his texts. I'm not strong enough.

He kisses my neck, causing my eyes to open in surprise. Then he bores those green eyes straight into my soul.

And his soul tells me the same thing it always does. That we should be together forever.

He breaks eye contact, holds his hands up, and says, "Boots, I give up."

"Then why are you here?"

He kisses me again.

This time with his tongue. That love-potion-infused tongue that always renders me incapable of speech.

He should've just used it the first time.

"You were right. It wasn't all about you. I jumped into relationships last year. I did things with girls I didn't have feelings for. I wanted to do things differently with you. And I know you loved the Keats guy. It was unfair of me to judge your relationship when I know nothing about it."

"But I can't—"

He kisses me again then says sternly, "I'm not finished yet." Then his voice softens. "Boots, I don't care about my past, or yours."

I study his face carefully, wishing it could be true. "Do you mean that?"

He gives me a teeny smirk. "Why, were you bad in the past?"

"Um, no," I say, carefully choosing my words. "I was just kind of a different person."

He cups my face in his hand, gazes into my eyes, and says sincerely, "I only care about your future. *Our* future."

"But sometimes people's pasts come back and ruin their futures."

"Not ours." He holds his palm up and says, "Don't move." Then he picks up a heavy shopping bag from one of the seats. "I got you something."

I watch as he reveals a large Mason jar.

I squint my eyes at it. "What's in there?"

"Dirt."

"You got me dirt?" I ask incredulously.

He grins, his green eyes sparkling. "Yes. To build our mansion of love on."

I try to pretend his reference to our love mansion doesn't affect me, even though it makes me completely melt inside. I manage to give him a chuckle and say, "It's gonna be a small mansion."

He laughs too, then looks at me seriously. "It's symbolic dirt. It also means a fresh start." He sets the dirt down on the floor between us, then puts his hand on the wall above my shoulder, boxing me in like he's done before. "I don't care if everything we've told each other up until this point is a lie. We start over. Here. Today. This second. Both of us.

On fresh dirt."

I can't speak. I can only look down at the jar of dirt—the non-sand dirt—and wonder how in the world he could possibly know the one thing that I so desperately need.

I'm lost in thought when he takes my hands in his, brings them to his lips, and asks gently, "Boots?"

Tears flood my eyes as my heart overrides my brain. I stare at the jar of dirt and say longingly, "I really want dirt."

"You want dirt?" Peyton asks loudly from behind us. "Are you serious? I told him that was the dumbest thing I've ever heard."

Aiden turns and glares at her.

She responds by miming zipping her lips and throwing away the key.

He turns back toward me and puts his forehead against mine. "We both need dirt. Please let me come with you."

Damn the gods, damn fate, damn everybody.

But I find myself nodding.

Nodding and crying.

I may not be able to give him my love, but I can give him the one thing I couldn't give anyone else.

Closure.

I'll let him come with me. I'll tell him on the island that I can't go back to Eastbrooke. That my mom is making me go to Vancouver or something. That maybe we can stay in touch. And if I survive my face-off with Vincent, maybe, someday, I could see him again and tell him the truth.

And I know it's selfish, but maybe there will even be a few more take-my-breath-away moments before I put him on the plane and send him back to school without me.

I'll tuck those moments away with the other ones I've had in my life and carry them with me while I fight Vincent.

The moments of a life that used to be.

His own eyes are teary as he uses his thumbs to brush away my tears. "Is that a yes?"

"Aiden?"

"What, baby?"

"I don't want to start over. Not completely. We've had too many amazing moments to forget."

The smile that spreads across his face could light up the heavens. It's full of emotion.

He hugs me tighter and gives me a kiss.

A true love, fairy-tale kind of kiss.

But I don't want to hurt him again.

"There's a lot going on in my life that you don't know about. I was actually looking forward to being alone. Trying to sort things out."

"There's a lot we need to talk about, but I'll give you whatever space you need."

"Fine. I'll let you and Peyton come with me."

"Good," he says, still running his hands slowly down the sides of my arms.

"Okay. So, uh, I should probably tell the attendant we're ready to go."

"Okay," he says, but he doesn't let me go.

He kisses me again.

After a long kiss, I let the flight attendant know that we're ready.

We get buckled into our seats and prepare for takeoff.

Peyton scrunches up her nose. "So, you liked the dirt?"

I let out a little chuckle. "No one but me would've liked the dirt."

She nods as she puts earbuds in, hits some music on her phone, and then leans back and closes her eyes. The flight attendant gives her a blanket right before we take off and she snuggles under it.

I grab my phone out of my bag and hold it up in front of Aiden's face. All of a sudden, I feel strong enough to know what he said.

He takes it out of my hand, turns it off, and puts it in his pocket. "You have to turn your phone off now."

AFTER WE GET to cruising altitude, I ask for it back.

He shakes his head at me. "No, I'm deleting them."

"But I wanna know what you said."

"I'd rather tell you. On the island, in front of the ocean; preferably after a couple tropical drinks."

"That bad?"

"Well, they started out with me trying to explain. Trying to understand. But then, toward the end, I'd say I was probably sounding pretty pathetic and desperate." He shakes his head and smiles at me. "I don't want to ruin my reputation."

I watch as he scrolls through my phone, frowning, shaking his head, and occasionally rolling his eyes at what he wrote. "Pathetic," he says, pressing buttons and deleting messages. When he's finished, he hands me back my phone. "Only left one," he says, putting his lips on my neck and grazing it with every syllable. "The most important one."

I look down at my phone and read.

Hottie God: *I'm not giving up on us. I can't give up on us.*

I'm really glad he can't see the emotion that's written across my face as I read. I close my eyes tightly and try to forget that in a few short days he's going to have to do just that.

"Do you care if I lie down and rest for a bit?" he asks.

"Uh, no. Go ahead," I tell him, but I'm not prepared for what he does. He stretches his long body out on the couch and puts his head in my lap.

I can't stop my fingers from running through his hair, moving gently across one slightly puffy eye, touching his adorable freckle, and skimming across his nose. I'm convinced now more than ever that he's a god with special healing powers, because his broken nose is still completely straight and beautiful.

He closes his eyes and quickly starts breathing heavily.

I remember when he was asleep in Bryce's room the night I saw his note, *Why should I bother?* And his answer, *Because she felt it too.* Back then I didn't think he was talking about me. Now, I think he was.

Oh, I never should've let him stay on this plane.

Telling him goodbye is going to be one of the hardest things I've ever had to do. Right up there with leaving my family and B.

But I'll just have to put on my big girl panties and do it. I want us to have an ending. I want him to be able to move on. To not have things up in the air the way they are with B.

I kiss his forehead, close my eyes, and try not to cry.

A FEW HOURS later, Peyton wakes up, stretches her arms above her head, unbuckles herself, and then comes to sit down next to me.

"We're a fun crowd, huh? I'm sorry I fell asleep." She looks down at Aiden sleeping in my lap. "He hasn't been sleeping much. Neither of us have."

"Why haven't you been sleeping?"

"What you did with Whitney. Sitting with her when no one else would. That's the kind of girl I used to be. I never wanted anyone to feel left out. I got so wrapped up in myself, it's embarrassing."

"Don't be embarrassed. When I told you it would backfire on you, I was speaking from experience."

"What happened?"

"Same deal. I started to worry more about my status than about people. I didn't like the way my best friend was behaving, so I decided to break away and make my own group. But I didn't go about it the right way. I didn't choose those friends very wisely. My big coup was throwing a skip-school party and not inviting her. She ended up sitting at lunch alone while we were sharing party pics. It didn't even really affect her, but I screwed up a friendship that was important to me, caused one of my friends to get drugged, and became a bigger bitch than she was. And even after that, she still helped me."

"We talked," she says, referring to Whitney.

"How'd it go?"

"Okay. I apologized for being an ass all year. I know she's always held that stuff over my head, but it's been a long time since she's threatened to use it. Probably just my own insecurities. I was shocked she did that to Chelsea. She's never done something like that for anyone. It's always been for herself."

"I think it was her warped way of apologizing for all the mean stuff she did to me. And if it's any consolation, she's just as screwed up as we are."

"You never seem to screw up." She looks at my hand still absentmindedly running through Aiden's hair. "Except maybe with him. He likes you."

"I like him too."

"If only it were still that easy," she laughs. "Like in middle school. All you have to say is she will like you if you like her back."

"That's funny."

She sighs. "What do you think of Camden?"

16

"I think deep down he's a good guy."

"I sometimes wonder what it'd be like to marry him. But I can't really picture it."

"Then it's probably not right," I say, my mind immediately conjuring up a wedding to Aiden. A hillside overlooking the ocean at sunset. Close friends and family. Ribbons in the trees and big hurricane lanterns lighting the aisle. Dinner at a winery. Brick patio. Candles on every surface and twinkle lights strung above our heads. Me in a dress with golden embroidery. Gorgeous shoes. Then a party. Dance floor set in the trees. Lots of wine. Lots of dancing. Aiden in a black suit looking a little dangerous and totally delectable.

Peyton touches my arm, causing my daydream to evaporate. "I just want you to know that when we go back to school, things'll be different. I'll be different."

I gave her an understanding nod.

Peyton and I have different backgrounds but we're alike in so many ways. I know with a little more time she could've been a lifelong friend.

Lifelong.

I know that once I start this showdown with Vincent my life might not be very long.

But, I guess, at least it will be mine.

"So, what are we gonna do on the island?" Peyton asks.

"Relax. It has everything you could possibly want. Aside from the ocean, sandy beach, and infinity pool, there is a two-lane bowling alley, gym, movie theater, and even a small nightclub."

"You and Aiden could dance. He said you guys had fun at the club in New York City."

"We did have fun. I loved the Empire State Building. Did he tell you we watched a couple get engaged?"

"He did. You know, he's gotten romantic."

"What do you mean *gotten*?"

"All the little things he's done for you. He's never really had to try with a girl, but your relationship is different. And what the hell was the dirt about?"

"You know how some relationships are kinda shallow? You like them because they're hot, or just for sex, or cuz you want to make someone jealous?"

"Yeah."

"He wants a relationship that's deeper. One that has a strong foundation. The dirt is supposed to be the start of it."

She sighs and clasps her hands together. "My parents have a relationship like that."

"My grandma told me this morning that she believes fate brings people into your life but it's up to you to decide who stays."

"I hope fate brings me a gorgeous, down-to-earth, soulful hottie."

"So did you have a Thanksgiving break back-up plan? Like, for where you were going if I said no?"

"I had one. Aiden didn't. Every time I brought it up, he told me no."

He's good at that word, I think.

"He said he couldn't entertain the thought of you saying no. That he had to focus on the positive. He's been a wreck, Keatyn. I've never seen him like this. No one has."

"It was a bad deal."

"But he didn't really do anything wrong. I don't get why you're still mad."

"I'm not mad."

"I know he's my brother and I'm biased, but he's a good guy. And I know that he's dated a lot of girls and I can see why that would upset you, but—"

I hold my hand up. "We'll figure things out."

"Fine. I'll let you two handle it. But I have some stuff that I need to say. Stuff I need to say out loud."

"Uh, okay."

"I've been living my life with a chip on my shoulder and using what happened to my mom as an excuse to justify my behavior."

"Have you forgiven yourself?"

"I'm trying. That's part of why I'm looking forward to this trip. It's a new beginning for me. Of living with the conscience I was raised with. And of figuring out what I want from life."

"Any ideas on that?"

"Well, I have enough credits to graduate in December. I'm thinking about doing it and taking some time off. It would mean missing soccer, but it's not like I want to play in college or anything, and I couldn't care less about missing Prom."

"So would you go home?"

"Maybe. Or get an apartment somewhere fun. New York or LA. Maybe start my own business."

"What kind of business?"

"Did you see the journal I made for Miss Tina?"

"With the cool cover? Yeah."

"I made it. Well, I handmade the paper that I covered it with. I'd love to do something like that. Make really cool paper designs and use them for journals, stationary, wallpaper, lampshades. Do you think I could major in papermaking?"

"I'm sure you could major in art. Do you think I could major in shoes?"

"Not acting?"

"Um, no." Here come the lies again. This is why I can't

go back. I'm sick of telling them. She's pouring her heart out to me, and I'm lying to her face.

Speaking of faces, Aiden's beautiful one has a little smirk on it, like he's having a good dream.

And it makes me feel even more determined to fight Vincent and defeat him.

Maybe I'll walk right into Vincent's office and say, *You want me? Here I am. Let's make your fucking movie.*

Then I'll see what he does. Maybe he's just a bully and the minute I stand up to him he'll back down.

Or maybe it would force him to actually make it.

And maybe he could have a freak accident with a lighting boom. Or maybe we could have someone tamper with his brakes. I could send him a note telling him to meet me up the beach. Curvy road, some rain, skidding off a cliff, and good riddance, Vincent.

"Have you ever made a guy bucket list?" Peyton asks me.

"Like all the different types of guys you want to be with?"

She laughs. "No. Like the qualities you want your dream guy to have."

"Um, not really. I mean, I've thought about it, but I've never written it down." Unless you count a script.

"I'm going to make a new bucket list for my life on this trip, and I'm going to rework my Mr. Dreamy List."

"Mr. Dreamy?"

"Yep. My list for my perfect man."

"What's on the list so far?"

"How we'll meet. Of course, it will be love at first sight. An instant amazing connection."

"What does he look like?"

"Kinda tall, in good shape, great arms, but not too

bulky."

"Kinda like your dad?"

She cocks her head. "I suppose so. Isn't that what every girl wants? To fall in love with someone like her daddy?"

I think about Tommy and sigh. "Yeah, kinda."

She keeps going. "I want him to look good but not be all about appearance—like, I don't want him to spend more time getting ready than I do."

I laugh, remembering Sander. "I dated a guy like that. I was jealous because his hair always looked better than mine."

"Exactly, and he needs to look good in the morning, like right when he wakes up. That's one thing that Camden had. That sexy morning scruff. How he looked even hotter when his hair was messed up."

"What else?"

"He'll love to travel, but like being at home too. We've traveled a lot with our parents but my best memories are of all of us at home doing nothing but hanging out. That's going on my new bucket list. I'm even giving it to my parents. They are amazing, but I think they've gone a little overboard on the whole experiences thing. They're missing moments with us." She looks down at Aiden. "You know, it's funny. He's my little brother, but he's the one who always takes care of me. He even had all those parties in his room to keep me out of trouble."

"I know."

"I'm glad he stopped. I need to keep myself out of trouble."

"So, back to Mr. Dreamy."

"I think abs are a given, right?"

"Definitely."

"And I think he'd be darker-haired but not dark and hairy. Like, maybe a guy who was blonde growing up but then his hair got darker."

"Cute," I say. "What will he be like personality wise?"

"I'm a Virgo. So, I'm pretty organized and structured. My mom says I need someone who isn't like that to balance me. Someone who's creative and free spirited. I don't really care, as long as he looks good in a suit. And maybe wants to get naughty on his desk," she says with a grin.

I think about Aiden pushing me on his desk, kissing me with his tongue, and setting my panties aflame. "I like guys who look hot in a suit. Getting naughty on a desk sounds fun too."

Aiden opens one eye. "Are you two talking about sex?"

Peyton giggles and covers her face with her hand.

"Speaking about talking, isn't that what we're supposed to be doing? Cuz if you aren't careful, you might just get voted off the island before we even get there."

He gives me an adorable grin as he sits up and wraps his arms around me. "You better not be serious."

"I think I'm just gonna go listen to some music," Peyton says, quickly taking a seat on the other side of the aisle.

Aiden leans over and kisses my nose.

"Stop that. It won't work on me."

He scrunches up his nose, then winces.

I touch it. "Did it hurt bad?"

He takes my hand and lays it over his heart. "Not as much as this did."

Shit. What am I going to tell him on Sunday? I'll have to come up with a good lie. One he can't counter.

"I never meant for you to get hurt, Aiden."

"When you came to my room, I said everything wrong. I was hung over, my face hurt, and I was so fucking pissed. Pissed that Chelsea said those things to you. Pissed that you believed her. Pissed that Riley broke my nose. Pissed he almost got expelled. Logan told me you asked him about the trigger that led to Maggie cheating on him. I know I was the trigger. I shouldn't have just said no. I should have talked to you about why I said no. It's just that saying no was hard for me. That's what I meant earlier when I said I give up. I'm not saying no anymore. But what I don't understand is why you wouldn't talk to me after. Why it felt like we were over. Why the chapel felt like goodbye."

Because it was, I think, as I press my fingers into the corners of my eyes, trying to get rid of my tears, and sigh. "I think I may be leaving Eastbrooke soon," I blubber. I can't bring myself to tell him *soon* means in just four days.

"Why? I thought you liked it."

"I love it."

"So, why leave?"

"I miss my family, Aiden. Going home for the birthday party was hard."

"Do you miss your family or miss your ex?"

"I miss everything."

The captain comes over the speaker and tells us to get buckled up for our descent into St. Croix, effectively ending our conversation.

MAKE A WISH.
5:30PM

WE GET PICKED up from the airport in the Morans' vintage Mercedes station wagon by a driver I have never met and who doesn't look like he belongs.

The driver opens the front passenger-side door and says in an authoritative tone, "Miss Monroe."

While he and Aiden load up our luggage, and he herds Aiden and Peyton into the backseat, I text Garrett.

Me: *Is The Crab's new driver one of yours?*

Garrett: *How did you know?*

Me: *His posture is too stiff for the islands, he's not very friendly, and he has no tan.*

Garrett: *I sent two men. They've fully briefed the usual staff about your situation and about how your friends don't know the old you. They have also removed all photographic evidence of you with your family.*

Me: *How did you know my friends ended up coming?*

Garrett: *Cooper was insistent that there be men at the airport. They were scrambling when you went inside the office.*

Me: *Oh. I just bought more hours.*

Garrett: *Yes, I heard. Planning on doing a lot of traveling in the near future?*

Me: *Maybe.*

Garrett: *Don't you dare take off on your own. You get your butt back to school when break is over.*

Me: *I'm not sure what I'm going to do.*

Garrett: *Tommy told me about your conversation. I agree with getting your mom and sisters to France, but why would you be ready to do a movie at Christmastime?*

Me: *Because I'm going to get my life back. Did he get Mom to agree?*

Garrett: *She agreed, but they still have to get out of her contracts. It's going to cost them a lot of money, but Tommy doesn't care. I'm flying to Nice on Friday to vet the security.*

Me: *OMG!! I'm so relieved.*

Garrett: *As am I. Your mom is a wreck.*

Me: *Make her feel safe, Garrett, and she'll get better.*

Garrett: *You can make us all feel better by not doing anything stupid. When you get back, I'll come to town and*

*we can discuss this plan of yours with Cooper. Because I
highly suspect Cooper knows nothing about it.*
Me: *I'm tired of lying.*
Garrett: *Don't do anything rash.*
Me: *Don't worry. Everything will be well thought out.*
Garrett: *That worries me more.*
Me: *I gotta go. I'll call you after the break. I promise.*

We enjoy the breathtakingly beautiful drive from the airport to The Crab, where we are greeted out front by the staff.

"Miss Keatyn," the long-time cook, Inga, says as she gives me a mama bear hug, "it's been too long."

I introduce Aiden and Peyton and then say, "I'll show them to their rooms now." As they follow me across the great room, I tell them, "After I show you to your rooms, go ahead and get unpacked, freshen up, and change. Then we'll meet back here and I'll give you the full tour."

Peyton stops at an expanse of glass to admire the ocean-front view and the infinity pool below. "This is beautiful," she says, jumping with excitement.

"Wait until you see your room," I reply, leading them both down the south breezeway to her guest suite.

"Oh, my gosh," she says, running from the view of her private tropical courtyard through one set of French doors to the view of the ocean through the other.

I press a button on the wall to light up a screen and quickly explain how to control her music, lighting, room temperature, and curtains, as well as send requests for food, drinks, or any amenity she might need.

"Your closet and bathroom are here," I say, opening the door to the bathroom that my mom describes as heaven on earth.

"This is amazing," she says in awe, standing in the middle of the bathroom and taking in the mirrored glass tiles that glitter from every corner of the room. The sleek, pale gray travertine that reflects the colors of the ocean. The spa tub that fills like a rain shower from the ceiling and has views of the ocean. The walk-in shower with its mosaic design on one side and its glass walls opening to her private courtyard on the other.

Aiden jokes, "We may never see her again."

"Wait until she smells all the food cooking. She'll wander out."

Peyton swats her brother but pulls me into a hug. "I can't thank you enough for letting us come here. This is so incredible." Then she goes over and plops down on her bed. "I'll meet you in an hour. Freshening up may take longer than I expected."

"You can come back through the breezeway or go out on your veranda, take the stairs down, and follow the path back."

Aiden grabs my hand as I lead him to his room. Even though we slept in the same bed at my loft, I didn't want to assume we would here, and now I'm glad I didn't because I need Aiden in his own room. I cannot fall asleep or wake up in his arms at any time during this trip. It will only make leaving that much harder.

I show him his suite. It's amazing too, but in a different way. It's decorated in a traditional British colonial style. Dark wood, pale blues, and amazing views of both mountains and ocean. It also happens to be conveniently located near the path leading to my room.

"This is great," he says, not really looking. "But I wanna go see your room."

"Don't you want to throw on a swimsuit or go to the bathroom or something?" I ask, hoping that he does. I have something that I need to go do by myself.

"I'll come back for my swimsuit," he says firmly.

"Uh, well, um, okay. Why don't you take that breeze-way there?" I say, pointing to the one that leads to the turret. "And I'll meet you there in a minute."

"Why can't I just walk with you?"

"Um, well, I have this thing I always do when I first get here. Kind of a tradition. So, I need to go do that and then I'll meet you there."

He takes my hand tightly in his, letting me know I'm not going anywhere without him.

"Fine," I say, rolling my eyes and quickly giving in.

I lead him out onto the veranda, down the stairs, and follow the path to the mermaid fountain.

"This is the fountain you told me about," he says excitedly.

"I always visit it when I first get here."

"Why?"

I take a couple of pennies from my purse and make a big gesture of handing him one, trying to convince him that this is just a fun, silly little thing I do.

"I make a wish," I say, avoiding Aiden's eyes as my voice betrays me by sounding hopelessly romantic. I turn toward the mermaid and her prince, close my eyes, toss my penny into the fountain, and make the same wish I always do.

I wish that someday I'll find my prince.

When I open my eyes, I notice that Aiden's still holding his penny. "Aren't you going to make a wish?"

He pulls me into his arms. "I'm standing here with you. I already got my wish."

I flash him a lame attempt at a smile. Why can't I hide my emotions around him? It's the same way with B. It's like they can both see right through my act.

"Do you always make the same wish?" he asks me.

"Um, yeah."

He nods and hands me his penny. "Take mine and wish for something new."

I look into his eyes and know exactly what he wants me to wish for.

Him.

But there's only one way that could ever be possible.

Aiden holds my hand—I think to give me extra luck—while I toss in the penny.

I wish I could have my life back.

After I open my eyes and watch the penny sink to the bottom, Aiden says, "So, let's see this room of yours."

I give the mosaic one last, fleeting look, then lead Aiden to the turret entrance, up the spiral wooden staircase, and to the big wooden door. I show him into the round suite with walls of stone, curved window seats, and views of the ocean in almost every direction.

"Wow," he says. "This is quite a view."

"You should see the bathroom," I say, pulling him into it. I show him the big tub that sits on a raised stone pedestal and how it opens up to the outdoors. I lead him out onto my curved balcony.

He looks down and laughs. "Rapunzel, Rapunzel, let down your hair."

I laugh too. "I used to stand up here when I was little and make my friend say just that."

He turns me back toward the bedroom. "You have a big bed," he says cutely, referring to what I said at my loft when I was trying to get him to share my room.

"I do," I reply, eyeing the king-sized four-poster bed draped with mosquito netting. "I also used to gather up every pillow in the place, stack them on this bed, and pretend I was the princess from *The Princess and the Pea*. That reminds me . . ." I walk over to the side table and open the drawer, just to make sure it's still there.

"What's that?"

I pull the thick book out and show him.

"Fairy tales, huh?"

My eyes get teary thinking about how that's all I've ever wanted.

My fairytale.

My prince.

My happily ever after.

But it all seems so silly now.

Because life is not a fairy tale.

In those stories, a prince never told the princess that he was gay. Or that it was her fault he got drugged. Or that he was going away for a year. Or that he got a text from his ex. And never did the princess have to put him on a plane and send him back to his castle. She never had to fight the dragon alone. And she never had to choose between two princes when the fight was over.

But, then, none of the princesses were stupid enough to make a wish on the moon.

Aiden gently takes the book out of my tight grip and sets it on the table. Then he sweeps me into a dance, humming a familiar song.

One of our songs.

I lean my head into his shoulder and enjoy the dance, knowing this will probably be our last. I try to tuck it away in my memory.

The way his body fits perfectly against mine.

The way his lips feel as they brush across my ear.

The way his hand is splayed possessively across my back.

He stops humming and whispers, "Let me sleep here

with you."

I stop moving and swallow. I can't.

I really can't.

But, oh, how I want him to hold me in his arms every second of each day I have left with him.

Even if it's nothing but pure torture.

A life-sized version of listening to our twenty-nine-song playlist over and over again.

"You told me you wouldn't say no," I reply, hoping that will force him back to his room.

"I won't. We can do it right here, right now, if you want to."

"I want to wait," I say. I can't be with him. I cannot be with him.

"Seriously?"

"I never wanted to have sex, Aiden. I just wanted to do a little more. And I hate being told no."

"That's a lesson I think I've learned," he says, touching his nose and laughing.

"You're going to have a little bump on the left side of your nose. Your face isn't going to be quite so perfect anymore."

"I'm far from perfect, Boots, but I know that I'm perfect for you."

My eyes fill with tears again and I can't help it. I kiss him.

Hard.

Full of passion.

Of regret.

Of I wish.

Of I'm going to cherish every single kiss for the next four days.

"Damn," he says ten minutes later, after he's pulled me

on the bed and I've finally stopped kissing him to breathe. He pushes my hair behind my ear and runs the back of his hand under my chin. "As much as I'd like to stay here and kiss you, we should probably go meet my sister."

"Yeah, you're right," I agree, pushing myself off the bed.

As I run into the bathroom and throw on a bikini, he asks me, "So what were you going to do here all by yourself?"

"I have a list."

"What's on it?"

As we walk hand in hand back to the main house, I tell him. "Just some stuff. It's kinda lame."

"Tell me anyway."

I roll my eyes and start reciting my list. "Eat a fish I caught myself was on there, but that sounds gross in retrospect. Do yoga in the sand. Swim with the dolphins."

"Will we see dolphins?"

"If we take the wave runners out and just sit there, we might."

"What else?"

"Macramé a pair of sandals." I laugh at myself. "I probably won't do that. I don't even know how to macramé. Let's see. Make a necklace out of shells. I do that every time I come here."

"I'd like a shell necklace," he says, pulling my hand to his lips and kissing it.

"We'll look for shells tonight," I say as we wander into the great room and find Peyton kicked back, tropical drink in hand, nibbling off a tray of snacks.

"You need to go change," she says to Aiden.

MY SURFBOARD.
8PM

I'VE GIVEN THEM the full tour, we've walked the beach, and we're now sitting poolside, having a drink and a few appetizers before dinner.

Aiden is telling us about his parents' Thanksgiving safari when Peyton says casually, "There's a guy walking up your beach with a surfboard." She takes another sip of her fruity umbrella drink then asks, "Do people surf at night?"

"Around sunset they do, but not usually in the dark," I reply, instantly panicking that Vincent has found me.

But then I turn around and see him.

He's walking up the sandy path, carrying a surfboard and looking like home.

"Oh my gosh! That's not just *any* surfboard! It's *my* surfboard!" I scream with delight.

I jump up and barrel towards him as he yells out, "Keats!"

I fling myself into his arms and plant a big kiss on him as he picks me up and twirls me around.

"I can't believe you're here!" I screech. "And you brought my board!"

When he drops me to my feet, I don't let go. The last time I saw him, I didn't hug him like I should have.

"I thought you were supposed to be here alone," he says.

Shit, I think, glancing back at Aiden and Peyton. *This* is going to be hard to explain.

"I was but they showed up at the plane and—wait, how did you get here? Do people know you're here? What if you were followed?"

"Calm down, Keats. I flew from Tokyo to LA. Went to my dad's. Even went to the Undertow and offered to play for them tomorrow night, knowing I wouldn't show up. Then I snuck over to your house and got your board. Glad no one's changed the garage code. Dad's assistant picked me up at the pier, drove me around in circles, and then to the airport where I hitched a ride with a company exec to North Carolina. In North Carolina, I had another plane waiting to bring me here. No one knows I'm here but B and Dad's assistant. Even my family thinks I'm home sleeping off jet lag."

"I'm so glad you're here."

"I'm glad I'm here too. Now for what's important. Tell me that incredible creature sitting on my deck is real and not an amazing jet-lag-induced mirage."

"She's real, Damian, but you can't."

"Oh, but I can. She has the most perfect lips."

"Ohmigawd, no. Don't look at her mouth. Don't even look at her. And don't talk to her at all."

"I'm not going to be rude to your friends."

"Don't you dare fall for her. You can't."

"Too late. She just smiled at me. I'm in love."

"Damian. No."

"Don't tell me no. Be nice. I went through a lot to get here so that you wouldn't be alone for the holiday. But, happily, you are not. And you even brought me a treat."

"She is not your treat, but I suppose I'm going to have to introduce you."

"Hell, yeah, you have to. I need to be introduced to my future wife."

I laugh at him and start to walk back, when Damian grabs my arm and says, "You forgetting something?"

"Oh my gosh! Yes, I am!" I walk back to him with a grin. I love this boy. Ever since the first time I came here when I was nine, he's given me a piggyback ride up to the house.

He drops my board in the sand as I jump onto his back and hang on tight.

He does his normal crazy gallop up to the house, trying to get me to fall, and then deposits me on the deck in front of Aiden and Peyton.

"So, this is my friend, Damian. He brought my surfboard," I say awkwardly, because I haven't had the chance to figure out exactly what to say. At school, no one can contradict my lies. Damian and I need to get our stories straight.

"Damian, this is Aiden," I say as the boys shake hands. "And his sister, Peyton."

Damian stares into her green eyes with an intensity I've never seen.

"Hi," she says, her voice cracking.

"It looks like I need a drink." He barely gets the words out of his mouth when Sven sets Damian's favorite pineapple rum drink in front of him. "It's good to be back home," Damian says.

"Home? As in, this is *your* home?" Aiden asks incredulously.

Damian nods.

"Where have you been?" Peyton asks him excitedly.

"Just traveling around," Damian answers cryptically. Does he not want Peyton to know he's in a band or is he worried about our cover story?

"Well, that's very specific," Aiden says in a condescending tone.

I look at Aiden. He's not relaxed anymore. His body is stiff and he's squeezing the life out of the napkin that was under his drink. Does he not like Damian? Is he mad that I gave him a big kiss on the cheek?

Damian glances at me, giving me his that-guy's-a-dick look.

"Tell them where you've been, Damian," I say, trying to ease the uncomfortable tension.

"Well, I recently had the pleasure of surfing all over the coast of Japan."

Aiden smashes his teeth together and pushes himself away from the table with so much force our drinks slosh all over. "Excuse me," he says and walks away.

Peyton looks at her brother with confusion as Damian says, "What's his problem?"

"Uh, I don't know." I get up and go after him.

He's marching quickly down the path Damian just walked up.

"Aiden, wait," I say, running behind him. When he turns around to face me, there's fire in his eyes.

"You seriously brought me on vacation to *his* house?"

"Um, yeah. He's a nice guy, Aiden. You should get to know him." I stare at him, not understanding why he's so pissed. "Why are you acting like this?"

"Is that the real reason you told us not to come? Because he decided to?"

"What? No! I didn't know he was coming, in case you couldn't tell by my happy screams of surprise."

"Of course. You're his Keats. He brings your surfboard and you forget all about me and the dirt."

"I haven't forgotten about you or the dirt—oh, wait! He's not *the* Keats guy."

"Bullshit!" Damian yells out from behind us.

"Shut up," I yell back.

"Don't let her give you any bullshit stories, man. I've *always* been the Keats guy."

I grab Aiden's arm and march him back to the deck,

saying to Damian, "Yes, you gave me the nickname, Keats. But I think he thinks you're B."

"Oh . . ." Damian says, finally getting it. He turns to Aiden. "Is that why you were being such a dick?" Aiden doesn't reply, so Damian stands up, pulls me close to him, and laughs. "I may not be *that* Keats guy, but I was the first guy to kiss her. When she was twelve. You can be jealous of that, if you want."

"But that's it," I quickly state.

"Yeah," Damian says, faking sadness and shaking his head in sorrow. "I was always her frog."

I smile at Damian. He's being adorable and Aiden has already unrolled his fists.

"She hates this," Damian says, then he licks his tongue up the entire side of my face and goes, "Ribbit!"

I playfully smack him, so he falls back into his chair.

I decide to tell them the story of how I know Damian. That way Damian and I will be on the same page. "I've known Damian since I was little. We went to school together and after my dad died, my mom wasn't coping very well, so the Morans invited us to come stay with them."

"Back then, it was nothing like what it is today," Damian adds.

"What was it like?" Peyton asks, batting her eyelashes at him.

"When Dad bought the property, it was a small resort. Six separate beach shacks, which eventually became pieces of the house you see today. The turret was originally on the neighboring property, but Keatyn and I were obsessed with it, so Dad bought it too. It was all that remained of a really old castle—which was home to either a Danish governor or pirates, depending on who tells the story. It was the first thing to get restored."

"The resort was named The Carib," I keep going. Loving that this conversation has morphed into one about the property. "Carib was a reference to the Native Indians who used to live on St. Croix. But Damian and I took the *i* out and dubbed it The Crab." I smile at Damian, remembering all the fun we've had here over the years. Back when my life was easy and carefree.

"So, pretty much anytime we came, we invited Keatyn and A—, her mom," he says, covering quickly. "Dad always said she kept me out of trouble. And she did. She was always making up plays and making me act them out."

I laugh. "I was sort of obsessed with the story of the frog prince."

"And Prince Eric and every other fairy tale."

Peyton stands up suddenly and grabs my arm. "Keatyn, come with me to get some drinks."

I'm about to tell her all she has to do is press the button on the digital screen sitting on the side table, but she whisks me inside before I can speak.

"Ohmigawd! I just figured it out!"

"Figured what out?" I say, trying to keep the panic out of my voice.

What did she figure out? That he almost said Abby? Or that Matt and my mom have worked together on movies for years?

"That's *Damian Moran.*"

I laugh with relief. "Um, yeah. I told you that."

"No, you introduced him as Damian and then you said something about the Morans. That means his dad is the director, Matt Moran? And he's *Twisted Dreams'* Damian?"

"Uh, yeah."

"But why didn't you say that you knew him when we were watching his video?"

"I think I did. You probably don't remember," I lie. "You were busy lusting over him. I told you we'd get tickets to his concert, remember?"

"Oh, yeah, I do remember that. Anyway. Oh. My. Gosh. He is so dreamy. And even cuter in real life! Do you think he'll sing for us?"

"Peyton, he just got off tour. I think he's looking forward to some down time. No screaming fans."

"Oh, of course he is. Shit." She runs her hands nervously down her cover-up. "Do I look okay?" She peeks in a mirrored surface on the bar. "Oh, my hair is a mess. Why didn't you tell me my hair's a mess?"

"Damian loves windblown hair." Shit. Why did I just say that? But it's fine. Knowing Peyton, she's probably just looking for a hookup.

"Did you see the way our eyes met? I swear, it was exactly how I pictured it would be with Mr. Dreamy. That instant connection. He's amazing."

Or not. Shit!

"Peyton, what do you mean? You don't even know him."

"So he's *not* amazing?"

"He's my best friend. Of course, he's amazing. I just mean . . ."

"Fine. I don't know him well enough yet to say, but seriously, I think I'm in love with him. He looked so sexy standing there . . ."

I tune out her gushing because they. Can. Not. Be. Together.

I picture it in my head. Vincent finding out Damian is dating some East Coast boarding school girl. He wonders how they met and immediately thinks of Miami. Of how Riley and Dallas were dressed in total prep. And then he comes to Eastbrooke looking for me. None of them would be safe.

"I think this calls for champagne," I say, grabbing a bottle out of the fridge, four flutes from the bar, and hitting a button on the wall.

Maybe the champagne will calm me down.

Sven comes out of the kitchen. "Yes, Miss Monroe?"

"We're having champagne to celebrate Damian's surprise arrival. Can we get a bucket of ice?"

"Of course. Would you like me to uncork it for you?"

"No, thanks. We'll do it."

"Very well. I'll bring the champagne stand out to the deck. Would you like to eat dinner poolside or on the screened veranda?"

"The veranda," I reply as he retreats to the butler's pantry.

"WE BROUGHT CHAMPAGNE," Peyton coos as she ditches her former seat for one on the couch next to Damian. I notice Damian's eyes lingering on her long legs.

I hand Aiden the bottle. "Would you like to do the honors? You did such a good job with it the last time we had champagne."

"And when was that?" Damian asks.

"They went to Keatyn's loft in New York City a few weeks ago," Peyton says dreamily as Damian squints at me. I shake my head slightly, letting him know that now is not the time for him to ask about the loft.

Aiden pops the champagne and we all stand as he fills our glasses. Then he raises his own in a toast. "*A thing of beauty is a joy forever: its loveliness increases; it will never pass into nothingness.*"

"That's beautiful," Peyton says as we clink glasses.

"And especially true, since we're surrounded by nothing but beauty," Damian says, holding Peyton's gaze.

I grasp my chair and slowly sit. My mind replays B saying the same quote right before he kissed me. And how he recently texted me the rest of the quote. How I used it in my script.

I'm really starting to hate poetry.

"More Keats, huh?" I say to Aiden while Peyton and Damian flirt.

"I realize it's risky, but it was one of the texts I sent you."

"You mean one of the texts that you deleted."

"Yes. I think I was somewhere between pathetic and desperate at that point."

"What do you think it means?"

He takes a swig of his champagne, like it will give him confidence, as Sven returns with the champagne bucket.

"Dinner is served on the veranda," he says. "Shall I move the champagne there?"

"Absolutely," Damian replies excitedly. "I'm starved. What's on the menu tonight?"

"Miss Monroe requested Kobe burgers—"

"With your homemade jerk sauce?" Damian interrupts.

"Of course," the butler replies, with mock indignation. "Inga wouldn't dare use anything else."

"And there's homemade French fries with her secret seasoned dip," I tell Damian. "Your favorite."

Peyton and Damian gather up their glasses and head toward the veranda.

Aiden grabs my pinkie with his. "I think it means that love is a thing of beauty. That it never fades away. I'm sorry I was a jerk. I just thought . . ."

"It's okay. You reacted and walked away," I say, suddenly feeling sad. Mostly because I know he's going to do the same thing in a few days. Only this time, he'll walk out of my life for good. "Why don't you go on to dinner? I don't want to leave my board outside. I'll just be a minute, but don't wait for me."

I turn and walk down to the sand, leaving Aiden standing there alone.

I PICK MY board up and lovingly wipe the sand off it. I remember practically passing out when B surprised me with it on my sixteenth birthday. How he told me I'd outgrown my beginner's board. I run my hand across the hot pink and orange graphics that he designed and notice something new. Running down one of the rails is a sticker in flowing script.

Life is divine chaos

I close my eyes, fighting back tears for the hundredth time today, and wonder when he added it. It had to be after he knew he was leaving, but before my party. It's exactly the kind of sweet thing he would've done. And I know exactly what I would've done once I'd seen it. I'd have taken my board out into the water and had a good cry; then I would've gotten my ass on a plane to wherever he was.

And, after hearing his side of the story, that's probably exactly what he had hoped for.

It would have been romantic and dramatic. An amazing script.

The problem is, I don't know how the story would've ended.

Would we have fought like we did in Europe and broken up for good? Or would we have ended up living happily ever after?

I carry my board to the storage area, standing it up next to the other surfboards and water toys. Before I leave, I run my fingers across the words and vow to bring chaos into Vincent's life.

I wander over to the veranda slowly, trying to compose myself. I see Aiden, Peyton, and Damian, all sitting around the big table, laughing and eating. Well, Peyton and Damian are laughing. Aiden seems to be lost in thought.

I feel bad about what I said about him walking away, because I know I would've done the exact same thing.

I give him a smile and sit down next to him. He puts his hand on my thigh under the table and gives it a squeeze. I know it's supposed to be a sweet, reassuring squeeze, but it doesn't comfort me.

It sends tingles across my body, causing me want to forget about tomorrow, drag him to my room, strip him naked, and dare him to say no to me again.

I eat a few fries and pick at my burger—two things I normally love—while carrying on polite table conversation. After Damian steals the last fry, he says, "Peyton, would you like to go for a walk on the beach?"

"I'd love to," she says in an unusually high-pitched voice.

She follows Damian toward the screen door but then stops and turns around.

"You guys want to join us?" she asks nicely, but I can tell it's the last thing she wants.

"Naw, you go," I tell her as Aiden says, "We should go."

"Why should we go?" I ask him as Peyton rushes to the beach without waiting for us.

"I can't just let my sister go out there with him alone.

She doesn't even know him."

"You don't have to worry about her being safe, Aiden. He's a great guy."

He squints his eyes at me, judging. "What does he do? Is he in school? Have a job?"

"Um, he's in a band called *Twisted Dreams*. They did a European tour this summer and then Japan this fall. And he got his GED so he could go on tour."

"So, does he hook up with girls on tour?"

Uh, yeah, I think, but I can't say that. "I don't think so."

Aiden rubs the side of his face. "You sure she'll be okay?"

"I promise."

"Fine. I'm really tired, anyway. I was hoping to head to bed soon."

"Bed?"

"Yes, bed," he says. "Come on, I'll walk you to your room."

"Um, are you tired?" I ask as we walk to the turret. Did he decide that he doesn't want to sleep with me?

When we get to my door, he gives me a kiss on the cheek. "Goodnight, then."

I nod at him, so he turns to walk away.

But I can't let him go.

"Aiden, I don't . . ."

"I don't want to be alone either," he says, quickly finishing my thought and hugging me tightly. "I know we have a lot to talk about, but when you came back from putting away your board, you seemed—I don't know—distant."

"We have all break to talk," I say, avoiding the inevitable. "And I'm just tired."

"It has been a really long day, Boots."

"I know," I reply as he opens the door and sees my room at night. The bedding is turned down and the candles in the hurricane lanterns on each side of the bed are lit. The screen door is pulled shut to keep out the bugs but allow the soothing ocean sounds in, and the sky is dotted with a million stars.

He looks around the room. "This is beautiful." He laughs. "I think I say that about everything when I'm with you." He pulls me onto the bed with him, kisses my shoulder, and then whispers in my ear, "You make every moment beautiful."

We lie down on the bed and I snuggle into his shoulder.

He doesn't talk, just gently strokes my hair.

I soak up his presence, trying to absorb everything that is Aiden into my memory. His dreamy scent. The way my head fits perfectly on his shoulder. How when I'm with him I feel like I'm in a bubble, safe and protected from the outside world.

Tears start sliding onto Aiden's chest before I can stop them.

"Baby, why are you crying?"

"Because I didn't think I'd ever get to lie in this spot again."

"You fit perfectly."

"I'm sure other girls have fit just fine."

"Maybe, that was BK."

"BK?"

"Yeah, Before Keatyn. Because since you came into my life, no one else fits."

"Aiden, why did you write on the moon?"

"I was trying to be poetic and tell you how I feel."

"So, you feel like the moon has been holding your dreams afar?"

"Lately, yes."

"Me too," I say, snuggling closer and quickly falling asleep.

Thursday, November 24th

THANKSGIVING DAY
WHAT IF BULLSHIT.
5:50AM

I WAKE UP when I realize I forgot to close the curtains before we went to sleep. It's dawn and there's a soft breeze flowing through the windows.

I slip out of bed carefully so that I don't wake Aiden. He makes a sleepy little moan, then rolls over onto his stomach as I hit the button to close the curtains so the sun won't wake him.

I head to the bathroom, throw on a bikini, and then wrap myself in one of the long teal cashmere robes that is a fixture in every room. Peeking back at Aiden, who seems to be sleeping soundly again, I sneak out to enjoy one of my favorite parts of the day when I'm at the beach.

I wander down the pathway to the sand, curl up in one of the big daybeds, and stare out at the ocean.

A little later, I hear the toy shed opening. I turn around and see Damian walking out with a surfboard.

"You're up early," he says to me.

"I forgot to close the curtains."

"My internal clock is on a different time zone. You wanna grab your board and go out with me?"

"Um, probably not," I say in a sad, pathetic voice.

Damian jams his board into sand. "What's your problem?" he asks in pissed off tone.

"I have a whole lot of problems, Damian. Which one are you referring to?"

"Well, that's one of them, right there. Last night you were crazy. Sometimes you seemed like you were ready to burst into tears. Other times you seemed pissed off at the world. Sometimes there were glimmers of a smile. And other times you acted like a big bitch, just like you are now."

"He put a sticker on my board," I say quietly.

"Aiden did?"

"No, B did. Sometime between when he told me he was leaving and my party."

"What's that got to do with anything?"

"He was telling me the truth. He did want to throw me in his suitcase and take me with him. And if I hadn't almost gotten kidnapped and left for Eastbrooke, the next time I surfed I would've seen the sticker and known. And I would have gone to wherever he was."

Damian grabs my wrists tightly. "This has to stop. All this *what if* bullshit. It's not your fault you were almost kidnapped by some psycho dude. You can only control *now*. The present. And *if* in the future you get your life back, *then* you can decide if you want to give B a chance. But until then, you need to live in the now. It's not every guy who gives you dirt, ya know."

"I only have seventy-nine hours left."

"Until what? Are you dying?" he says in a panic.

"No, although it feels like part of me is. I have seventy-nine hours left until I end it with Aiden. I'm not going back to Eastbrooke."

"Where are you going?"

"I don't know yet. Somewhere I can hide out while I try to take over Vincent's company."

"You need to go back. You're safe there."

"I have a feeling that when this all goes down it will not be pretty. Seriously, Damian, it might all blow up in my face. That's why Peyton needs to be *just* a fling."

"But, if you're not going back, I could date her."

"If he found out you were together and that I went to Eastbrooke, neither one of you would be safe. Don't do that to her, Damian. Don't put her in that kind of danger."

"I have a better idea. You go back and I'll keep our relationship a secret."

"Your *relationship*? Damian, you've known her for less than twenty-four hours."

"And it only took about two seconds of those hours for me to know. All of a sudden, I'm a fate loving, love-at-first-sight believing, fairy-tales-can-happen kind of guy."

"That sounds like a song."

"Speaking of songs, I'm writing one. I've never felt more inspired. Everything looks prettier with her in the picture."

"Aren't you going on tour again?"

He gives me a smart-ass grin. "Studio time. Recording a new album, then touring the good ole U.S. of A. And I was thinking this morning, Dad's got a sweet apartment in New York City that I've never taken advantage of, and with my stepmom pregnant, they won't be using it any time soon."

"Your dad and Tommy start filming the third *Trinity* movie there in December."

"Shit. Well, it's a big place. Or maybe I'll just get a little apartment near your school."

I raise an eyebrow at him.

"Fine. I'm being impetuous and crazy. But come on, Keats, you've know me forever. Have you ever seen me like this?"

"No. But maybe you're just sick of groupies and craving a girlfriend. It doesn't mean she's the one. You're barely eighteen."

He shakes his head and squints his eyes at me. "No, don't say that. *You* of all people. Maybe Vincent changed your life, but don't you dare let him change who you are. You should be clapping and jumping with excitement. You should have a huge smile on your face and that dreamy look in your eyes." He pulls me up off the daybed and twirls us around in a circle. "Be happy for me. Be excited. Be your usual hopeless romantic self. Write me a script where I'm the prince and not the frog. Make a wish on the moon. Or a shooting star. Or at 11:11. Throw a penny in the fountain. Tell me you saw the green flash."

Tears flow from my eyes as I remember my old self. The girl who saw possibilities instead of roadblocks. The girl who believed in fairy tales and wishes.

We stop spinning and both drop dizzily back onto the daybed.

"I've been trying not to, Damian," I say, wiping my tears. "But I can't pretend. This is my reality. Vincent was there when I went to see B surf. When I saw my mom in New York. When I went to Vancouver. My drama teacher almost invited him to my school so I could audition for his movie. You don't understand. I can *never* let my guard down. I have to monitor *every* word I say. Think about *every* move I make. I *can't* live in the moment anymore."

"Maybe you can't at school, but you can here."

I shake my head. "I wish I could, but when Peyton told me some guy was walking up the beach, my first thought was that it was him."

Damian nods. "Okay. I get it. But I'm here now. So I want you to let go and at least enjoy your next seventy-nine hours. Stop holding Aiden at arm's length and let him in."

"What about B?"

Damian frowns and furrows his eyebrows. "Fine. You want reality? Here's reality. B cares about you. But he chose his dream over you."

"That sounds so harsh."

"It's supposed to be harsh. It's the truth."

"But he said . . ."

"What he said doesn't matter right now because you can't be with him. So, move on. Besides, it's Thanksgiving. You should be thinking about what you're thankful for."

"I'm thankful for you, Damian." I get tears in my eyes again. "I'm sorry. I swear, all I do is cry anymore. But I really am glad you're here. And I'm glad you met Peyton. So, if after this weekend you still want to see her, you can have my loft."

"Yeah, what's that all about? You bought a loft and didn't tell me?"

"I didn't tell anyone from my old life; not even my mom. I needed somewhere safe to go." I smile. "It's a really awesome place. You'll love it."

"So, is that where you're gonna fight Vincent from?"

"Oh, no. I can't go back. I took Aiden there and he . . . well, he infused it with love potion."

"Love potion?"

"He has special powers."

Damian doesn't look convinced. "Like what?"

"When he's around, my head feels like it's filled with cotton candy and I can't think. His smile is as bright as the sun. He knows what I'm thinking even before I can think it.

I'm almost positive his tongue is infused with love potion. You should be careful because I think his sister might have . . ."

"Her tongue is definitely infused with love potion," he says dreamily.

"Damian, how do you know that?"

"We hung out last night."

"Did you sleep with her?"

"No, I was a gentleman and dropped her off at her door, where I kissed the hell out of her. And then I couldn't sleep. Which is why I'm up so fucking early. I wish she'd just wake up already. Shouldn't she be dying to see me?"

"Text her."

"And say what? *Wake the fuck up so I can see that gorgeous smile again?*"

"That'd work for me."

He smiles and pulls out his phone. "I'm going to text her and you're going to do two things. The first one is to stop blaming yourself."

"And the second?"

"March your ass to Aiden's room and start living in the present."

I nod, agreeing with him. "You're right. I shouldn't waste what little time I have left with him."

"Exactly. So go wake him up and let's have some fun."

"I'm gonna run up to the house and get him breakfast; then I'll see if he wants to surf with us. I don't know if he even knows how."

WHEN I GET in the house, I find Peyton in the kitchen, pouring herself a glass of orange juice and smiling at her phone.

"Have you seen Aiden?" she asks with a smirk. "I don't

think his bed was slept in last night."

"It wasn't. He stayed with me."

"Ooh la la."

"It's not like that. We're not having sex."

"I bet you do before this trip is over." She waggles her eyebrows up and down and grins.

"No, we won't."

"Is that what the dirt means? Taking it slow?"

"That's part of it, yeah."

She sighs as she picks up a muffin and examines it.

"It's coconut-banana with an orange glaze."

"Yum," she says, putting it on her plate. "I've never really taken it slow before. Damian seems like he's a gentleman."

"I take it he didn't jump your bones last night?"

"It's not just that but, like, he held the door open for me when we went outside. He has great posture. And last night, there was this big moth and he kinda protected me from it. He just has this presence—like, he makes me feel safe." She smiles. "He even walked me to my door last night. We kissed," she says slowly touching her lips. "It was . . ."

Damian sneaks up behind her, kisses her cheek, and finishes her sentence. "The best kiss of her life."

She smiles and playfully slaps his arm. "I wasn't going to say that."

Damian grabs her, tickles her sides, and pulls her into a chair with him. She squirms around, laughing and screaming, but then Damian stops her screaming with his lips.

They kiss.

And kiss.

And keep kissing.

"Uh, I'm gonna go take Aiden some breakfast," I say,

even though I'm ignored.

DIE BY THE WAVE.
6:40AM

I SET AIDEN'S food on the nightstand and then gently perch on the edge of the bed.

He's still lying on his stomach and I can't help but admire his muscular back, the adorable way his buff arm is curled under his head, and the sexy scruff trailing across his cheek.

I reach out and run my hand through his soft hair.

He opens his eyes slowly and sits up. "Mhmm. I was just having the best dream."

"I'm sorry I woke you, then."

He quickly pulls me into his chest and kisses the top of my head. "Don't be. This is even better than the dream."

"I was going to let you sleep in, but Damian wants to surf. Have you ever surfed before?"

"No, I never have."

"Well, then either I can teach you, you can watch, or you can eat and go back to sleep. I brought you a smoothie and a couple homemade granola bars. When we're done surfing, Inga is making Damian's favorite breakfast."

"What's the favorite breakfast?" he asks, while taking a drink of his raspberry-coconut smoothie.

"Homemade cinnamon waffles drizzled with her amazing pecan caramel sauce and spicy fried potatoes. The combination of the spicy and sweet is to die for."

"That sounds really good."

I snuggle closer to him and close my eyes. "Aiden, I'm

sorry about yesterday. My emotions were kinda all over the place."

"It's okay. Mine were too." He rubs his palm down my arm. "I was afraid you'd kick me off the plane, then I was so happy you didn't, then I was pissed when I thought Damian was your ex. Then, after you put your board away, you seemed really distant. But what you said about being afraid you'd never lay on my shoulder again made it all worth it. I went to sleep feeling quite content."

I laugh. "Sounds to me like your feelings were feeling complicated."

"Exactly," he says with a laugh as he rolls on top of me and kisses me with lips that taste of raspberry.

After a thorough kiss, he leans his elbow above my head. "We were supposed to talk on the plane."

"Do you still want to?"

"That all depends," he says, his fingers making a lazy trail down the side of my neck. "In forty years are you going to dredge it back up?"

"If I do, I won't be mad about it anymore." I picture myself watching Aiden forty years from now, dressed in jeans and dusty cowboy boots, his dark blond hair starting to gray at the temples, those bright green eyes still speaking to my soul as he wanders onto our front porch, our grandchildren in tow, their hands and mouths full of dark red grapes they just picked from the vineyard.

"Promise?" he says, those green eyes asking way more about what the promise implies.

I can think of a million reasons why I won't even know Aiden forty years from now, but I can't make myself say anything but, "I promise."

"So let's focus on the positive."

"Right," I agree, willing myself to let go and live in the

now. At least for the next seventy-some hours. "It's Thanksgiving Day. We're together in paradise, and we have a busy day."

"A busy day? I thought we were supposed to be relaxing."

"We will be, but there's a lot to do here. Surf. Eat. Lie in the sun. Eat more."

"You forgot something important," he says as he curls his hand into my robe and draws me in closer. "This is soft."

"What'd I forget?"

"Kissing."

Then he kisses me until I can't think straight.

Eventually, I force myself to say, "We're supposed to be out surfing. You need to go get your suit on."

He reluctantly nods, but then gives me another electrifying kiss.

The kind of kiss that infuses me with so much more than love potion.

It infuses me with hope.

AIDEN FOLLOWS ME to the storage shed so I can outfit him with a board.

"I'm going to start you out on this board. It's a little bigger and more forgiving when you're learning."

He grabs the board and says, "Great. Let's get out in the water."

"Not so fast." I look at the board, knowing it hasn't been used in a while. "Run your hand over the surface here where you're going to be laying. Do you feel anything?"

He wipes his hand across the board. "Nope. Is that good?"

"Not really. It's way too slick. We need to wax it first." I grab a square piece of wax, break it in half, hand it to him, and then lay our boards across a pair of sawhorses. I rub both boards down with a soft cloth to clean them and then say, "Okay, so first, you're going to just rub it back and forth like this. Just a little. Not using much pressure. I like just a thin coat."

He mimics what I do. "Got it. Is this how everyone does it?"

"No, it's just how I like mine. You use different types of wax depending on the temperature of the water, but everyone has their own way to do it. Some use special tools to put the wax on, some just use the wax like we are. Some layer it differently. But the goal is the same. The wax gives you grip."

"When I was learning how to skateboard, my dad stapled sandpaper over the top of mine."

"Exactly, that's the same idea. Only with wax, you can still see the cool design of your board."

"Yours is really cool."

"Thanks. It's custom. Fit to my weight, height, and abilities."

"And the design?"

I lower my head and press on my wax with a little more intensity. "Okay, so now you're going to do this. Make Xs or crosshatching across your board. From rail to rail. Just in this area here where you will lay and stand. And then a little more right up here on the rail where you'll place your hands while getting up."

I see Aiden's shadow fall across my board then his finger is under my chin, pushing it up so I have to look at him. "And the design?" he asks again.

"The Keats guy had it custom-made for my sixteenth birthday."

"Is that why you were upset last night? It reminds you of

him?"

I sigh. "No, that wasn't it, exactly."

He doesn't give up. "What upset you, then? Exactly?"

I run my hand across the sticker. "This sticker is new. It matches our tattoos. The chaos."

"Life is divine chaos," he reads and nods his head in agreement. "That's true. You never know what's going to happen next. Like, with my mom's cancer. Life was crazy, chaotic, and scary. But out of all that came something divine. She got her life back and is happier than she's ever been."

"She must be a really strong person. I don't know if I could be that strong."

"She considered fighting cancer like fighting a war with a worthy opponent, but one that was not invincible. You're stronger than you know, Boots, and if you ever have to fight something, I'm confident you'll be able to handle it."

I look down and slide the wax across my board again. I'm probably putting way too much on, but I don't care because I'm too busy praying that he's right.

"Okay, then!" I say with fake excitement. "Let's get you out in the sand!"

"Don't you mean water?"

"Nope, you gotta practice getting up on the board first. Lots easier to figure that out on the sand than in the water like I did." I set my board down in the sand and he follows suit. "So, lie down on the board like this; then, when you're ready, pop up like this into a standing position." I sit down on my board and give him a smirk. "Now, drop and give me twenty."

Aiden salutes me, then drops back down onto the board. I watch as he fluidly pops up to a standing position. As he counts down from twenty to one, I'm wishing I had told him to do a hundred. When he lies down on the board, he places his arms in front of him, like he's going to do a push up. This causes his shoulder muscles to ripple, his biceps to flex, and makes me wish I could slide under him every time he drops back down onto the board. He moves fluidly and effortlessly, his coordinated body doing exactly what he expects of it.

By the time he's counted down to one, he's starting to sweat. Little beads of perspiration are glistening across his chest. A thin line of water is running between his tight pecs and through a set of luscious abs. I want to grab his hips in my hands and run my tongue along the deep vee that continues down, just below his low-riding shorts.

I remember the first time I saw him. Yeah, my original observation was dead on. He is *so* the God of all Hotties.

"How'd I do? Am I ready for the water?"

"I'm definitely ready," I say, still thinking about my body under his . . . Oh, gosh. "I, uh, meant that I'm hot." For you. "And ready to get out in the, uh . . ." What's that big body of water called again? Oh! "The, uh, ocean. You know, get my surf on."

Oh my gosh. I am so lame. Excuse me while I go bury myself in the sand.

He grabs his board and follows me and my bright red face out into the water. Peyton and Damian are already out there, although it appears they're doing nothing but sitting on their boards, splashing each other, and playing kissy face.

"It's about time," Damian says. "Ready to put on a show?"

"Don't be a show off. I wanna teach Aiden to surf."

"Looks like you got the kiddie class, dude," Damian says, rolling his eye at Aiden. "You ride a snowboard?"

"Absolutely. It's one of my favorite things to do."

I turn my head at stare at him. "Really?"

He shrugs his shoulders, like I should've known that, but gives my hand a reassuring caress, telling me he can handle it.

"C'mon," Damian says, paddling out. "Live by the wave. Die by the wave."

"I don't want to die by the wave," I tell him.

"There are worse ways to die," he says pointedly.

I swallow, thinking of Vincent. "Yeah, I guess."

"You're totally slowing my roll with the death talk," Aiden says in a stoner voice, laughing.

Which makes me giggle like I'm high too. High on being in the water with Aiden.

Who would have thought?

"Just follow my lead," Damian tells Aiden as he takes the first wave and slices through the water toward shore.

"You don't have to do that curvy stuff. Just ride straight in."

Aiden chooses a wave, quickly stands up—his foot placement looking like it belongs in a surfing textbook—and easily rides the small wave into the shore.

I wait for a bigger one, eager to show off my skills, and feel the rush as I push up off the board . . . but then my hand slides off the edge of it, and I crash chin first into my board.

Shit that hurt, I think as the wave crashes on top of me and a riptide pulls me under. I let my body go limp trying to make myself float back to the surface so I can tread water. When I get back to the top, I see that I'm a lot further away from shore than I expected. Damian and Aiden are both wading through the waves frantically searching for me.

I try to yell that I'm okay, but end up coughing up some water. So I just wave my hand and let the waves carry me back to shore.

"What the hell was that?" Damian yells, pulling me out of the water and yanking the leash off my ankle.

"I forgot to put wax on the side of the rail. I slipped. It's no big deal."

"I couldn't find you," Damian says, still yelling at me.

"I'm sorry. What do you want me to do? You're the one who said die by the wave. Maybe you jinxed me."

Aiden touches my face gently. "You scared us both. And you have a little cut on your chin."

Damian is still pissed. Full of adrenaline. I can see that I scared both of them. Aiden is just handling it better.

I touch Damian's forearm. "It's okay. I'm fine. I've had way worse crashes than that. It was just a stupid thing made worse by the undertow. If you fall, be careful."

Peyton, who had rushed into the shed, comes back with a band-aid for my chin. "Here."

"Thanks. Does it need this?"

"It's bleeding. I'd think so. We don't want you attracting a shark, too."

I laugh. "No, we don't."

"Here. Let me put it on you. Your hands are all wet." She tears the sides off the band-aid and places it on my chin. I'm sure I look like an even bigger loser than I did when I crashed.

I push the band-aid in place, grab my board, add some wax to the rail, and head back out in the water. I know the best thing to do after a crash is get back out there.

The next wave I catch is different. It loves me. Big, broad crest that I'm able to carve my way up and down.

"That was amazing!" Aiden tells me, pulling me into his arms. "You're really good. I kinda thought after you crashed that you were maybe overstating your abilities."

"You thought I was bragging?"

He kisses my nose. "Maybe. Kinda."

Then he kisses my lips. And my band-aid. "Life with you is never going to be boring."

MEANING IN EVERYTHING.
10AM

AFTER SURFING, WE dry off and head in for breakfast.

I'm sitting at the breakfast bar watching Inga make her special caramel sauce.

"I've tried making that for Damian before, but I can never seem to get it right. The brown sugar always gets lumpy."

"Are you mixing it in the right order?"

"Yeah, kinda. Well, honestly, no, I sorta just put all the ingredients in at once and let them melt."

"You can't do that. You have to mix the brown sugar and butter first before you can add the cream."

I scowl. "Oh, yeah, I don't do it that way."

"That's because you don't like to wait, Miss Keatyn. You want everything now. You need to stop being so impatient and let life come to you. You're young; you have a lot of life left."

I know she's talking about being patient in cooking but what she says touches me deeply.

"Do you think that's true? That I will have a long life?"

She looks surprised at me. "Has Inga never read your palm?"

"Um, no. You always said I was too young."

She grabs my hand and turns it over.

Then a curious look crosses her face. "Very odd."

She lets go of my hand and pulls the reading glasses she wears around her neck up to her face. Then she looks more closely, studying my hand and tracing the line. Grabbing my other hand and comparing the two, she says, "It is believed that your dominant hand shows what is and your non-dominant hand shows what could be."

"So what do mine say?"

She runs her finger next to a line. "This is your life line. See this? How it is a chain up here at the top?"

"Yes."

That means things have been difficult for you early in your life. You lost your father, no?"

"Yes. When I was eight."

"But this. This split. It is unusual to see in someone so young."

"Why?"

"It means death."

"Death?"

"Yes, you cheated death, somehow. Have you had a brush with death recently?"

"She just about drowned," Peyton says, but Damian is looking at me with huge eyes and thinking the same thing I am. That if Vincent had actually kidnapped me, I'd be dead.

"Maybe it means I'm going to die soon," I say softly, knowing it could happen.

"No, it is in the past."

"How do you know that?"

"I just do."

"Uh, okay."

"But see how this strong thin line starts after the break?"

"Yes."

"It's a split or changed life. It often means the death of a spouse. A divorce. Something in your life has changed. This feels almost like a rebirth."

I think about my changed name. My changed life. I know I'm not supposed to believe in this stuff, but still.

"And after that?"

"This line is extremely chained at the beginning, so you'll have a difficult struggle during this rebirth, but then it emerges as a strong long line."

"What does that mean?"

"You will have a long, happy life once you get through it."

I put my head down, pretending to be inspecting my palm, but trying to hide my reaction.

Inga has no idea the overwhelming feeling of hope she's just given me.

"Do you want me to do the rest?"

"Yes, please," I mutter out.

"This is your heart line," she says, drawing her finger across it. "It's long, meaning you will be content in love. And this line is your head line. There are Xs in the middle. Here. That means you'll soon have to make a momentous decision. One that will affect the course of your life."

"Okay," I nod, wondering if she's referring to the decision I've already made. Not going back to Eastbrooke and starting to wage war on Vincent.

"See how these lines are connected at the top?"

"Yes."

"They mean you developed your aspirations early on in your life." She looks up at me. "Based on all the plays you and Damian have done here in the past, I'm assuming that means you belong in the entertainment industry."

"Uh, that's interesting." I don't want to talk about that possibly, so I try to get her to move on quickly. "What else do you see?"

"Based on the shape and length of your palm and fingers, I'd say you're very perceptive, sympathetic, and quite creative."

I smile. I love being those things.

"On the downside," she says, "you can be moody, emotional, and inhibited."

Damian and Aiden both start laughing. Damian says, "Emotional is right. I never knew a person who could have so many emotions at once."

Inga chastises Damian. "That's because she's perceptive, Damian. They go hand in hand."

I give Damian a smug smile but then squint my eyes at Aiden. "Why were you laughing?"

"Because you are the least inhibited person I know."

Inga also gives him the eye then says, "Inhibited can have many meanings, young man. Possibly she is emotionally inhibited, as I would suspect is the case based on what I see."

"Uh, oh. I didn't think of it that way," Aiden replies respectfully.

"The universe is a mysterious place and there is meaning in everything," she says confidently. She lets go of my hand to stir the caramel sauce and then returns to the island and grins at me. "Now for the fun part."

"What's the fun part?"

"How many children you will have, of course. You know that your mother's hand was very clear on that. She didn't believe me when I told her she would have five more children after you."

"Five?"

"Six total. One, which is you, then a large space, which meant the age gap between you and her second child would be large, then five lines close together."

"I'd love to have another sister," I say happily. But then reality hits, and I want to cry at the thought of not being there.

Just another reason to get my life back as fast as I can.

"So how many kids will Keatyn have?" Aiden asks with a sparkle in his eye.

"Hmmm. You will have four children very close together. See how these lines touch at the bottom?"

"Yeah," Aiden says, studying my faint lines very intently. "Twins."

"That's really cool," Aiden says. Then, turning to Peyton, "I always wished we had a bigger family."

"Not me," Peyton says. "I only want one kid. And I want to spoil her rotten."

"Rotten, is not good, Miss Peyton. Let me see your hand."

Peyton holds her palm up.

Inga shakes her head. "You should start mentally preparing. You are destined to have three boys."

We all laugh as Inga stops the entertainment and pulls our waffles out of the oven.

OBSESSION WITH FAIRY TALES.
11AM

AFTER CHOWING DOWN breakfast, we head back to the beach. We all play around on our surfboards and Peyton manages to get up on hers. She and Damian are constantly flirting and looking for any excuse to touch each other.

Aiden says to Damian, "I noticed you have a wakeboard

in the shed."

"Yeah," Damian replies. "We can get the wave runner out and I'll pull you around."

"That'd be awesome!"

"I think that's my cue to put my board away and spend some time tanning," I announce.

"That's what I want to do too," Peyton says. "I'm really wet."

I see Damian lick his lips. He so just thought something naughty. He grabs her around the waist and pulls her in for a kiss. "I'll miss you," he says in a lovesick way.

Oh, he's got it bad.

Peyton giggles uncontrollably. In fact, she's still giggling when we lie on two of the cushioned chaises that line a small portion of the beach.

"I don't think I've ever seen you giggle so much."

She giggles again. "I'm, like, giddy and having so much fun. Damian is sweet." She stops and studies me. "Is he sweet? Please say he's sweet."

"Yeah, he's super sweet."

"It's silly isn't it? He's practically a rock star. Travels all over. I'm still in school. He's younger than me. And probably into groupies."

"He looks really good in a suit," I say with a smirk.

"He has pretty much *everything* on my list and the things he doesn't have I don't care about anymore. I'm falling way too fast. Hell, who am I kidding? I'm not falling, I've fallen. I need to stop it. Stuff like this only happens in the movies. But he's so hot. But in a different way. Like his face is beautiful but it's more classic. Have you ever noticed how perfectly proportioned it is?"

"Uh, I don't think so."

"He's just as hot as Cam, only I don't think he realizes

how hot he is. Like Cam works it. Uses his looks."

"Damian uses his words," I say softly. "His music. His voice, like when he whispers or sings you to sleep, it's completely dreamy."

"Great. So everyone who he whispers to falls in love with him?"

"I think anyone that hears him sing falls a little in love with him. With both his voice and his passion. He's also really mature. He never acted like a kid even when we were kids. He's always been, like, an old soul or something. He doesn't make the kind of mistakes I always seem to make."

"So he is perfect." She sighs sadly. "And he'd probably hate me if he knew all the mistakes I've made."

I know that I should tell her she's right. I know I should stop this relationship before it catches flight, but I can't do it. I can't crush this. I mean, Damian is the one who suggested Eastbrooke that night. Maybe fate sent me there for him. So that he could meet his dream girl. And if I'm not going back anyway . . .

"Peyton, what was your plan when you met Mr. Dreamy?"

"What do you mean?"

"What was your plan? After your eyes met and you determined he was the one, then what?"

She rolls her eyes. "We lived happily ever after, of course."

"What else?"

"You mean in between that? I guess I always imagined being courted in that old fashioned way. Wooed. Flowers. Romantic dates. Wondering when I'd get that next kiss."

"Did you ever think you'd sit around trying to come up with excuses why you shouldn't be with him?"

"Of course not." She smirks. "Oh, I see what you're

doing there. You're right. I should enjoy it. Speaking of that, I'm gonna run in the house real quick. And you should watch my brother. I think he's showing off for you."

I glance out at the ocean and see Aiden doing a flip on the wakeboard.

He tries another one, crashes, then gets pulled back up. He jumps the waves, getting a ton of air, and doing tricks. Turning around backwards, grabbing his board as he jumps, kicking his board up behind his butt, and doing more flips.

AFTER SHOWING OFF for a long time, he strides out of the water, plops his wet, glistening body on top of me, and gives me a steamy kiss.

"What's that for?"

"I want you to know how I feel. And right now, I feel exhilarated."

"Showing off exhilarates you?"

He grins. "Jumping the wakes and getting all that air is kinda a rush."

"Is there anything you can't do?"

"Speak French."

"Besides that?"

"I can't read your mind. You need to start telling me what you're thinking. Even if you think I can't handle it."

"I think you could handle anything," I say dreamily.

Although the feel of his hard, wet body on top of mine makes me want to pretend to be an evil queen and banish him to my turret room.

Forever.

"So tell me what you're thinking right now," he says, killing my daydream of him tied to my bed.

"I don't think you want to know what I'm thinking."

"But I do."

"Don't say I didn't warn you. What I'm thinking is that I hate you."

He kisses my neck, his mouth feeling cool from the ocean. "I'm lying on top of you, practically attacking you, and that's what you're thinking?"

"Yeah. Do you know how many freaking times it took me before I could ride into shore? I don't think I ever would've gotten it right if B hadn't come out and helped me," I stupidly blurt out.

"Who's B?"

"Oh. Um, he's the Keats guy. My stepdad gave me my first board, a few pointers, and then told me the best way to learn was just go out and do it. He was wrong, by the way. It's much easier to learn what to do on shore first. Anyway, that's how B became my first big crush."

"And your first big love."

"Yeah."

"Do you still love him?"

"Sometimes I think I do."

"And other times?" he says, his eyes holding mine.

"I think I'm falling for someone else," I say breathlessly.

Ohmigawd! I can't believe I just said that.

Why did I say that?

Why would I do that to him?

Give him hope just to crush him in a few days.

God, I suck.

"So is there anything you've ever wanted do that you haven't been able to do?" I ask, steering the conversation back to his athletic abilities.

He rolls over, positioning himself next to me, and looks at me with fiery eyes.

"There are a lot of things I want to do that I haven't done yet."

"Like what?" I reply, praying it's something like skydiving or mountain climbing.

"I've been dreaming of slowly undressing you."

I stop breathing for a second as my heart jumps into my throat. "Is that something you'd like to do soon?"

He rolls me to face him, while gliding his hand downward over my hip and thigh. Then he parts my legs with his knee, putting it in the spot he does when we dance, intertwining our bodies. Then he grabs my ass and guides it even closer, my crotch now firmly pushing on his thigh.

"Yes, very soon. And I want to be just like this," he says, placing his mouth on my neck. "Only naked."

I grab the hair at the back of his head and pull his face toward me so I can kiss him.

When his tongue takes possession of my mouth, I groan, my body purposefully pressing into his.

Damian yells from the water, "Dude, it's my turn on the wakeboard. Come drive for me."

Aiden ignores him, choosing instead to slide his tongue across my lips.

Then he says, "I suppose I better go."

I'm too breathless from the kiss to even reply. I just sort of nod.

God, he is hot.

And I don't just mean the way he looks.

It's that strong, almost alpha male, possessiveness that I feel when he's determined. An electrical charge backed by godly powers.

Like he's a human version of Poseidon's trident.

Aiden gets up and yells at Damian. "I'm gonna grab some water. I'll be right back."

"Grab me one too," Damian says.

As Aiden runs up to the pool bar, Damian pulls the

wave runner up into the sand, hops off it, and then plops down next to me.

"Jeez, when I said you should have some fun, I didn't mean you should accost the poor boy on the beach."

"Jealous?"

"Totally. Peyton has the best ass. I want to own it. Explore its surrounding areas."

I laugh. "You need to stay out of that part of town." He laughs, although I'm pretty sure he's completely serious, so I say, "Damian, if you really like her, shouldn't you want to take it slow?"

"I am taking it slow because what I really want to do is wave one of your magic wands, make you disappear, and throw her across a chaise and fuck her until she can't move."

"Damian!"

"Come on, don't pretend like you don't want Aiden to do that to you. You two have so much chemistry if you don't do it pretty soon you may combust and kill us all."

That makes me laugh. "Maybe, but if she's really your future wife, you should wait a little. I mean, what would you tell your kids?"

"I'd tell them Mom's ass looked so good in her bikini I couldn't help myself. My sons will understand."

"And your daughters?"

"We're not having daughters if Inga's palm reading isn't total bullshit. But if we did, I'd tell them the love at first sight story. Perpetuate the future generation's obsession with fairy tales." He grins at me. "Maybe I'd even tell them she was a mermaid."

I smack him. "Very funny."

"Do you think your mom and Tommy waited?"

"Ha. No. I'm pretty sure they did it on their first date. But, then, if a guy as hot as Tommy took me and my daughter on a private jet to a Russian ballet, I wouldn't have waited either."

"You and Aiden remind me of them."

"What did you mean?"

"When you aren't obsessing about your lack of a future and let yourself have fun, you just glow. Hell, you both glow."

"Do you like him?"

"Yeah, Keats, I like him. But just as a forewarning, don't plan on us hanging out tonight. I'm taking Peyton on our first date."

"Where are you going?"

"We're gonna take the jeep, drive up the mountain, and look for shooting stars."

"In the words of your father, *So you're taking her parking?*"

He laughs out loud. "Oh my gosh. I about died when he said that to us in front of everyone. I'm sure I looked completely guilty."

"We both did. The funny thing is that never once crossed my mind."

"That's because you were hell-bent on acting out some script you were writing. Where they laid on top of a mountain, held hands, and made wishes on shooting stars."

"That seems like a long time ago."

"Things were just simpler then."

"Yeah, they were," I say quietly, biting my lower lip.

"No. No. No. Don't start with the pout."

Aiden comes back, tosses Damian a bottle of water, and says to me, "Why are you pouting?"

"Because I'm taking your sister out tonight. She's jealous."

"Jealous?" Aiden says, looking a little confused.

"She loves looking at the stars."

"I'm sure we can find some stars of our own," Aiden says, kissing my cheek before running back out into the water with Damian.

PEYTON COMES WANDERING back out to our chaises with Sven in tow. She's carrying a laptop and Sven has two of his wickedly strong hurricane drinks on a tray. He sets them on a side table next to us and then heads back into the house.

"These drinks are really strong," I tell her.

"Perfect. I need to relax. I can't relax around him. It's like I'm strung out, waiting for the next hit. The next kiss."

"If you break into song about how his love is your drug, I may have to smack you."

She laughs, sipping and watching Damian on the wakeboard. "Wow, he's good on that thing. Almost as good as Aiden. I wouldn't think a guy who plays guitar would be so athletic."

"Damian is like Aiden. There isn't anything he can't do if he puts his mind to it." I laugh. "It pissed me off when we were younger. I was always trying to keep up with him. So what's the computer for?"

"Tell me that you have internet here and that you won't laugh at what I'm about to do."

"We have internet. The password is *crabbypatties.* And I'll try not to laugh."

She types on the laptop. "I'm about to match our horoscopes, so I need to know his birthday."

I laugh, not because I think it's funny but because I did the exact same thing when I was crushing on B. Horoscope matches. Magic 8 Ball questions. Fortune cookies. Numerology. Anything to give me hope that we might be together someday.

"You're laughing," she says, scrunching up her nose at me.

"Only because I've done the same thing when obsessed with a boy."

"Okay," she says clicking away. "I'm a Virgo and he's a, what?"

"An Aquarius. Smart. Creative. A little bit temperamental."

"Hmm," she says. "This says that when Virgo and Aquarius team up they can either bring out the best or worst in each other. It seems I tend to have a rigid and theoretical approach to life."

"Do you?"

"Yeah, I'm big on theory. And list making. And I need a certain order in my life to function."

I watch Damian out on the wakeboard, cutting as hard as he can across the wake and then racing up the side of the wave runner, trying to get ahead of Aiden. He's going balls out. Not once thinking about anything other than the rush. "Damian isn't that way at all. He's the anti-list maker."

"This says that Aquarians are poetic." She pauses. "I guess that would fit since songs are basically poetry. Oh, here. It says that we can thrive on our differences and grow together as we learn about each other. That's romantic, right?"

"Yes, it's romantic. What else does it say?"

"It says he's passionate, modern, hates routine, and seeks spiritual enlightenment, but that he can be opinionated and stubborn."

"Wow. That's pretty much on target, except it makes it sound like he's kind of a slacker. And he's not. He's highly motivated."

"Oh, my gosh. Listen to the end. The most positive

aspect of their union is that their combined ambition can drive them to do miraculous things together. Their relationship is enlightening and full of pleasure."

"I think the pleasure is referring to the mental kind," I say as I watch Peyton lick her lips.

"He's got amazing arms, don't you think?" she asks dreamily.

I look at his biceps flexing to hold the rope. "Yeah, he's got great arms. All that guitar playing, I suppose. And he loves to golf."

"Really?" she says, her eyes getting big. "Me too. Well, I like to drive the beer cart." She stops staring dreamily at him and says, "Okay, let's match you and Aiden."

"Oh, no. That's okay. I don't even know his sign."

"Luckily, I do. Did you know on his birthday he'll be eighteen? And that I'm already nineteen?"

"No, I didn't know that."

"We don't really tell people."

"Why? Were you held back?"

"In a way. We missed a year of school when my mom got cancer. It was the worst year of my life for lots of reasons. I was scared she'd die. Pissed I had to leave my friends and move to California. Although the worst part was watching her lose her hair. She had the most beautiful hair. Anyway, we're both a year behind. It was that year that made me put *Go to boarding school* on my bucket list. I couldn't handle it like Aiden could."

I look at Aiden driving the wave runner, laughing, and having a great time. He now appears to be on a mission to make Damian crash. He's driving in tight circles and trying to whip him around like you would to get someone off an inner tube.

"He didn't tell me."

"I know. He doesn't like to talk about it either. All right, so what's your sign?"

"I'm a Leo."

"L-e-o," she says as she types. "And he's a Sag-it-tar-ius."

"He is?" I say in shock. I seriously never would have guessed that. And I know every single Sagittarius quality by heart, because I've studied B's horoscope more than I have my own.

"Oh, wow. Listen to this! When you get together the result is usually fireworks. You are both dynamic and like to enjoy life to the fullest. As a couple, you are lots of fun to be around. And you encourage each other. And even though the Sagittarius' philosophical ways can compete with Leo's love of all things material and bigger than life, they can still get along. They admire and respect each other and together they radiate energy."

"That's okay, you don't have to keep reading," I say. "I get it. We're a good match."

"But there's so much more," she says excitedly. "It says the Sagittarius' sign is an archer, meaning he goes slowly and likes to take his time surveying his target. Oh, and he's a flirt. It says you might be bothered by that though because you like to be admired. It also says it will be a relationship full of passion and heat. So you're a good match horoscopi-cally."

"Is that a word?"

"Ha. I have no idea. But you know what I mean. It also says here that Leos sometimes pout to get their way. Do you do that?"

"Of course not," I say shaking my head.

"She's lying," Damian says, suddenly standing in front of me. "What are you two doing?"

"Nothing!" Peyton says, her eyes big as she slams the

laptop shut. "Just girl talk."

"Did you girls realize it's two-thirty already and almost time for Thanksgiving dinner?"

"Uh, no," Peyton says. "What time is dinner?"

"It's at three. And we can't be late."

"Oh, I better go get ready. What are you wearing, Keatyn?"

I grab her arm. "Come with me. I have the perfect dress for you to wear."

"Meet us in the great room, boys," I say with a wave to Damian and Aiden.

I pretend to be just taking her up to get a dress, but internally I am freaking out.

I assumed because B and I we were so perfectly matched it meant he was my destiny. I mean, we fell in love at first sight, *and* we were perfectly cosmically matched. We were made for each other.

But so is Aiden?

I drag Peyton up to my room trying to just focus on clothing.

I take her into my closet and pull out the gorgeous red slip dress I bought back when my goal was to seduce Aiden. "Here, wear this."

I hand her a strapless bra and the dress.

When she puts it on, she goes, "Wow. Just the way this dress glides over my skin feels sexy."

"You look amazing, but the bra looks bad. You may have to take it off."

"I can't go braless."

"Just try it." She undoes the bra and pulls it out from underneath the dress. "Now, look."

"I feel so sexy. Like, I've never really wanted to be sexy before. More like I just wanted to look hot, you know?"

"Yeah, I know. Did you bring some strappy sandals?"

"I have a pair of silver heels."

"Perfect, but just carry them. Set them on the floor next to you. You'll totally look casual but, yet, amazing."

"Okay, I'm going to go put on a little makeup. I'll meet you in the great room."

She stops, gets tears in her eyes, and looks at me. Then she rushes back to me and gives me a tight hug. "Thank you for bringing me here and for the dress. I've never been so happy in my life."

"Just have fun tonight. He's taking you somewhere special."

"That's what he said, but he won't tell me where. Seriously, I feel like I've walked into a fairytale. Hell, I'm even getting dressed in a flipping turret."

"Go finish getting ready, so you'll look perfect," I say, escorting her to the door.

Once I close it, I sit on my bed and stare at the computer she left behind.

Yes. I'm a glutton for punishment.

But I can't stop myself.

I open it and type in our match on a different website hoping to get a different result.

And I do.

But this one is worse.

As a lover, the Sagittarius man likes to explore his lover's mind, body, and soul.

I shut the computer and focus on getting ready.

I quickly shower off then throw on a soft crepe halter dress with an ombre wash that variegates from a pale pink at the neck and to a deep orange at the hem. I pair it with white studded double strapped platform wedges.

My mind suddenly flashes to Aiden taking this dress

slowly off me.

I close my eyes and indulge my mind for a few seconds before focusing on looking amazing.

I braided my hair while it was wet and let it dry in the sun, so I unbraid it, gently run my fingers through the soft waves and then add some balm to make it shine.

I stand back and study myself in the mirror. My face is tan and glowing, so I decide to skip foundation and blush and just add some sparkly pink eye shadow, a thin swoop of black liner, a bunch of mascara, and a peachy lipgloss.

I check the time and, seeing that I have a few minutes to spare, decide to check my phone.

There are texts from all of the Johnson boys, Maggie & Logan, Annie, and Katie, all wishing me a Happy Thanksgiving. But it's Dallas' text that cracks me up.

Dallas: *Would it be in bad taste if I offered to share my wishbone with the governor's hot 16-year-old daughter?*
Me: *You always can make me laugh. I love that about you. Happy Thanksgiving. Let me know if she decides to, uh, make a wish.*

It's noon in Vancouver, so I decide to call my family. I remember last Thanksgiving. The girls running around in little pilgrim headbands. Gracie wanting Tommy to buy her a pet turkey.

The phone is answered with, "Bonjour."

"Well, bonjour to you. Is this Avery?"

"Kiki?!"

"Hi, sweetie. I just called to tell you Happy Thanksgiving. Are you going to eat lots of turkey and stuffing today?"

She lets out a big sigh. "We were supposed to."

"What happened?"

"Bad Kiki jumped up on the kitchen island and ate the

turkey while we were setting the table."

"Oh, no! I bet Daddy was mad."

"He said *merde*. That's a bad word."

"Yes, it is. Why are you speaking French today?"

"I'm practicing. We're moving to France!"

I let out a huge sigh of relief, knowing that Mom would never tell the girls unless it was a sure thing.

"That's amazing! You'll love it there."

"Mommy says we'll get to go to the store, and to the beach, and to the park there! We don't get to here."

"That will be so much fun. Can I talk to your sisters?"

"Sure! I'll go get them."

I hear her running through the house, her little bare feet padding across the hardwood floors. I swear, this time next year, I'll be with them. No matter what.

I hear a chorus of, "Kiki!!" and "Happy Turkey Day, Kiki!"

Then, "Gracie, don't grab the phone out of my hands! It's rude!"

Then Gracie's sweet little voice, "I miss my Good Kiki."

"I miss you too, Gracie. I heard the puppy was naughty and ate your turkey."

Gracie laughs. "Daddy was chasing after Bad Kiki and she had bones in her mouth. I laugh and laugh at Daddy and Kiki."

"It bet it was funny. How's Mommy?"

"She's sick."

"Sick?"

"Yes, she in bed wiff the flu."

"Can I talk to her?"

"She sleeping. Daddy say, *Girls, be quiet*. But Daddy yelled at Kiki."

"Where's Kiki now?"

"Under Gracie's bed. She know it safe cuz Gracie love her Bad Kiki. Daddy say Kiki might not go to France and Gracie cry and tell Daddy, Bad Kiki no go, Gracie no go."

I can't help but laugh. I so wish I were there, because even though the house is always filled with chaos, it's like the perfect chaos. I hope Inga was right. I pray I live a long life and have a houseful of my own kids someday.

"Keatyn?" a deep voice asks.

"Hey, Tommy. Happy Thanksgiving. The girls said they're moving to France."

"Happy Thanksgiving to you too, baby. Tell me you're with some friends and not all alone."

"I'm with some friends, Tommy."

He lets out a sigh. "Good. One less thing to worry about."

"Is Mom okay?"

"Oh, yeah, just a flu. Everyone on set has been sick."

"Okay, good. I heard the dog ate the turkey."

"Damn dog. She's lucky she's so cute and Gracie loves her so much."

"I gotta go eat dinner, but tell Mom I love and miss her. And tell her next year things will be different."

"I hope you're right," he says, and then we say goodbye.

I don't know what's wrong with me. It's like I have pre-traumatic death syndrome or something. Every time I think of my future, I picture me dead.

Which makes me feel guilty, because I know Cooper's Thanksgiving has to be rougher than mine.

Me: *I was thinking of you today. I know it's gotta be rough.*

Cooper: *I was thinking of you today too.*

Me: *Don't worry about me.*

Cooper: *Garrett says you're not going back to school.*

Me: *I was going to discuss my plan with you after the holiday.*

Cooper: *Tell me now.*

Me: *Um, it's still in the planning stages, that's why I want to talk to you.*

Cooper: *Yet it sounds like you've made up your mind.*

Me: *I have about school. I just haven't decided for sure where I'm going to live.*

Cooper: *Don't take off on your own.*

Me: *I wasn't planning to. I was going to ask you to come with me.*

Cooper: *See, you're smarter than Garrett thinks.*

Me: *He thinks I'm going to do something stupid.*

Cooper: *Are you?*

Me: *I considered walking into Vincent's office and telling him I want to audition for his movie.*

Cooper: *Tell me you scrapped that plan.*

Me: *Not quite yet. I wanted to get your thoughts. He's like a bully, Cooper. Maybe I just need to stand up to him.*

Cooper: *There is a big difference between a bully and a sociopath. Do some research.*

Me: *Does that mean if I don't go back to school, you'll still help me?*

Cooper: *Of course.*

Me: *That makes me cry, Cooper. Thank you. I just want to be proactive instead of sitting around waiting for him to find me.*

Cooper: *Go eat some turkey. I heard your dinner smells amazing.*

Me: *Have you been keeping tabs on me?*

Cooper: *Absolutely.*

LOVE SONG ABOUT HER LIPS.
3:15PM

DAMIAN AND I are the first ones in the great room.

"This is crazy," Damian says, pacing in front of me, holding a glass of wine. "I'm insanely crazy about her. I'm currently writing the world's longest love song about her lips. She doesn't have a boyfriend or anything does she?"

"I don't think she'd be kissing you if she did."

"Trust me. That doesn't stop a lot of girls."

I touch his forearm and get him to look at me. "Damian, she felt it too."

His eyes widen in shock.

"Seriously? Do you think that really happens?" He sets his wineglass down without taking a sip of it and starts pacing again. "Of course, it happens. How many times have we heard the story of Ab—" He stops in the middle of his sentence, looking like a deer caught in the headlights, when Aiden walks in the room. "Um, the story of Aberly and, uh, Fritz."

"Who's Aberly and Fritz?" Aiden asks.

"They're my dad's friends," Damian says, picking his goblet up and taking a swig before continuing. "I need something stronger than this. You like scotch, Aiden?"

"My dad is trying to teach me to appreciate it," Aiden replies. "So tell us their story."

As Damian plunks ice into two highball glasses and pours a 25-year old scotch over them, he says, "They come here sometimes, and they like to tell the story of how they met. Of how it was an instant, love at first sight thing. They've been together ever since."

I smile thinking about Tommy and my mom. "Yeah, they're pretty amazing. I hope you can meet them someday."

Because I do.

I think Tommy would love Aiden, and my mom would be as mesmerized by him and his wooing as I am. I think about Logan and his big gesture. About Aiden and the dirt. B and his sandycastles. My mom is into big gestures, and Tommy never does anything small. He whisked her away to St. Petersburg on their/our first date. And a few months later, he surprised both of us by remembering the day my dad died, by taking us to his grave and then later to the Santa Monica Pier. He's never been threatened by our past, I think, because he's confident he'll be in our future.

Damian hands Aiden his drink as Peyton walks into the room.

She looks gorgeous.

Damian is staring at her, mesmerized. When she smiles the blazing love god smile, I see the same dreamy look in Damian's eyes that I suspect is in my own when I look at Aiden.

Speaking of Aiden. He looks gorgeous too. His hair is slicked back, making it look darker. The scruff on his face is looking sexy as hell over his tanned face. He's wearing a Rag & Bone pale blue gauze long-sleeved shirt, a pair of James Perse linen pants, and Prada criss-cross sandals.

Damian holds out his elbow to Peyton, whispers something in her ear that makes her blush, and then escorts her into the dining room.

Dinner smells fabulous, but looking at Aiden makes me hungry for only one thing.

Him.

Aiden grabs my hand, gives me a kiss, and leads me into the dining room.

WE INVITE INGA and Sven to join us for dinner, but as is

typical, they refuse. However, it's mostly because they're leaving early tonight to go to their daughter's home for a family birthday celebration.

As Sven pours us each a cool glass of Pinot Grigio to compliment the turkey, he says, "Mr. Damian, I assume you will keep with tradition and do your father's usual toast?"

Damian looks at me and smiles. "Keats, I think you should do it."

"Um, okay." I stand up, smooth down the front of my dress, and raise my glass into the air. "It's times like these that we stop to reflect on our lives. On the things we have to be thankful for. The great Thornton Wilder wrote, 'We can only be said to be alive in those moments when our hearts are conscious of our treasures.' In other words, look at the friends gathered around you, at the food sitting before you, and the beauty that is around you. Happy Thanksgiving!"

We clink glasses and everyone says, *Happy Thanksgiving*.

"That's a beautiful quote," Peyton says. "What's it from?"

"It's from the play, *The Woman of Andros*," I tell her. "It's about what's precious in life and how harsh the world can be. Wilder revisited that theme again in *Our Town*, when Emily dies and asks if anyone ever realizes what they have in life, while they are living it."

Aiden and Peyton both look teary-eyed. I know they're thinking about their mom and how even though she is with them, she's not with them. In a way, cancer was sort of their Vincent, bringing chaos into their normal lives. "I'm very thankful to be here," Peyton says. "Thanks so much for having us."

"So, do you both like football?" I ask.

"Well, my parents are both originally from Georgia, but my mom went to college at Alabama and Dad went to Ole

Miss. They're big SEC rivals, so football is a dangerous subject at our house," Aiden says with a grin. "It's always funny when the two teams play each other."

"How did they meet?" Damian asks.

"Dad interviewed Mom for a job. Their running joke is that he told her no for the job, but asked if she would interview to be his girlfriend."

"What'd she say?"

"That she'd rather have the job," Peyton says with an easy laugh.

"The Cowboys always play on Thanksgiving Day. Do you like them?" I ask. "My grandpa lives in Texas and is a huge Cowboys fan."

"I just like stuffing myself with turkey and then relaxing on the couch and watching any game," Aiden says. "Although, here, I think I'd rather hang out on the beach."

"You two enjoy," Damian says, before stuffing his mouth with mashed potatoes. "I'm going to take Peyton into town after dinner."

"Are you going shopping?" I ask, my ears perking up.

"Just some exploring and then we have our date," Damian says very vaguely.

I get the distinct impression that I'm not invited.

"Exploring, where?" Aiden asks.

"Just into town."

"Somewhere safe?"

"Um, yeah, of course."

Aiden nods and says, "Okay."

VERY QUICKLY, WE'RE stuffed, and Aiden and Damian are both moaning that they couldn't possibly eat another bite.

Until Inga offers them a piece of pecan pie and they both are like, *Oh, maybe just a little slice.*

Peyton and I help clear the table, but Inga shoos us out of her kitchen.

Damian grabs Peyton's hand. "Don't wait up," he tells me with a big grin on his face.

Aiden smiles at me, rubs his tight stomach, and pulls me into a hug. "Alone at last."

"Do you want to go down to the little beach cabana? It's shaded and has a comfortable bed that's great for naps."

"That sounds perfect," he replies.

We walk hand in hand to the beach and snuggle up on the raised platform bed filled with brightly colored pillows. I lean on Aiden's chest and stare out at the water in a happy food coma.

YOUR LIPS ON MINE.
8:45PM

"HEY, BOOTS," AIDEN says, waking me up.

"Oh, wow. Did you fall asleep too?"

"Absolutely."

I snuggle into his arms, my ear on his chest, hearing the beat of the heart I'm going to break along with my own in just two days.

"We were up early."

"And we played hard," he says with a grin.

"What time is it?"

He glances at his watch. "Almost nine."

"Oh my gosh, we slept forever."

"And believe it or not, I'm hungry again."

"Let's get a snack and take it back to my room."

He touches the strings of my halter. "I was serious when

I said I wanted to undress you."

I hold my breath as he touches my shoulder. There's a huge part of me that wants to skip the snack but, yet, I want to take it slow. Enjoy the whole night. The whole experience. Savor it like it's my last meal.

We head to the kitchen and make turkey sandwiches and then I grab one of the trays of cheese and fruit that Inga always leaves in the fridge for late night snacks.

"Do you want some wine?" he asks.

"Sure, pick something out."

WE WALK TO the turret, into my room, and then set everything up on the desk.

I throw open the windows, so we can hear the sounds of the ocean, and light the candles.

"I really liked your toast today," Aiden says.

"Thanks, I didn't make it up or anything but I think it's a good thing to hear on Thanksgiving. It helps put your life in perspective. I think it's easy to get so caught up in the everyday stuff that we forget to look at what's really important."

"What's really important to you?"

"Same as everyone, I guess. Health, family, love."

"I agree. Although I might add a few things to that list."

"Like what?"

"The sound of the ocean, watching the sun set, a good glass of wine, and your lips on mine."

"The simple things in life are the best."

"As long at it includes a castle on the beach, Little Mermaid?"

"I don't really need a castle, Aiden, but I do need the ocean every so often. The waves calm me and make me feel peaceful—centered, almost."

"You seem like that in your loft too."

"I do," I say with regret, knowing I won't ever be going back there. That I'll be hiring people to pack up everything and put it in storage. Except for two things. The book of Keats poetry, which has Aiden's four-leaf clover pressed in it, and the shoes I wore to my birthday party. Those will be sent to wherever I am. "Really, I'm comfortable lots of places. I love the vibrancy of cities like New York and Paris just as much as the ease of a house on the beach or in the country. I don't really know where I want to live."

Or even if I'll live.

"What's that?" Aiden asks, holding up his hand and walking over to the window.

"What's what?" I ask, following him.

"Shhh."

I listen quietly and then hear it. Giggling.

"Where's it coming from?" I whisper.

Aiden nods in the direction of the beach.

I peer out into the moonlight, and see Peyton and Damian stripping off their clothes and running into the ocean.

"Are they skinny-dipping?" Aiden asks, looking slightly horrified.

"Oh, no. I'm sure they have swimsuits on. Damian likes to swim in the moonlight," I lie.

"I think I should go down there and check on her."

"Aiden, you don't need to check on her. She's laughing and having fun."

"That's what I'm afraid of."

"You got to know Damian today. Do you like him?"

"Yeah, I like him. But that doesn't mean I want him getting naked with my sister."

I give him a kiss and say, "Let's go back inside."

Aiden studies my face. "You know, you've surprised me on this trip."

"How so?"

"Because we haven't done anything other than kiss."

"We were tired last night."

"Are we tired tonight?"

"No, we just took a nap."

He studies my bare shoulders and then runs his hands across them. "You're right," he says, his eyes dark and sexy. "We should go back inside."

He pulls me through the doorway, closes the curtains, and then comes to stand directly in front of me.

I bite the edge of my lip, knowing this is it.

He wants to undress me.

I stand here, feeling like I'm already naked.

He wraps his hand around my neck and unties the halter, causing the front of my dress to fall down and reveal my strapless bra. He bends slightly, his lips pressing against my shoulder, slowly across my collarbone, and then along the edges of my bra.

"I've had dreams about doing this. Just undressing you."

I swallow hard and my stomach flips as his hands slide down my sides, slowly working the dress over my hips, down my legs, and into a puddle on the floor. He bends down, stopping to trail his tongue across the top of my thong, then runs his hands slowly down the sides of my thighs, his lips following them.

He stops to take my dress from around my ankles and lay it on the bench at the bottom of the bed.

But then he returns to my legs, kissing my knees, my ankles, and removing my shoes.

His lips work their way back up to my mouth and, as he kisses me, I start to unbutton his soft shirt.

One button.

Two buttons.

Three buttons.

Four.

Part of me wants to pop the bottoms off the rest of his shirt, strip off the rest of his clothes and go for it, but I also don't want to miss this.

This slow burn.

My lips find their way to his chest as I finish unbuttoning his shirt and slowly spread it open, letting it reveal his muscular chest and beautifully sculpted shoulders.

It's magical. Godlike.

Until his shirt gets stuck on his hand.

I start laughing, because it won't come off no matter how hard I tug on it.

He pulls the sleeve back on, showing me that his watch is in the way.

I nod in understanding, unbutton his sleeve, and then pull it off him.

Then I put the shirt on me.

"Something is wrong with this picture here," he teases, gliding his finger down my stomach. "My clothes are coming off and you're putting them back on."

"This shirt is soft. I might steal it and wear it to bed." I sorta hug myself and run my hands down the sleeves.

He growls a little. "Are you going to take off my pants?"

My face instantly flushes—hell, my whole body instantly flushes.

I nod and move my hands to his belt while he pulls the shirt off my shoulder and kisses down my chest.

They are slow, soft, controlled kisses.

As he's doing that, I unbuckle his belt.

Then I unzip his pants and let them glide down his legs

into a pile at his feet.

"Sliders, huh?"

"Yeah, they're comfortable."

"And way hotter than boxers," I state. Because those things are tight. As in, I can see the outline of every bulge underneath, including the one muscle I've been dying to see.

But I remind myself that the sliders must stay on.

Do not take off the sliders.

Do not pull off the sliders.

He quickly kicks his pants off, and then in one fluid motion picks me up and lays me on the bed.

"I have a present for you," I tell him, having no idea why I chose this moment to bring it up. Especially when I should be focusing on what I can feel under those sliders.

He props his head up, his green eyes sparkling in the candlelight and possibly looking the sexiest I've ever seen. "Really?"

"I was going to give it to you when you passed French this semester."

"But you're so confident that I'm going to pass that you're giving it to me now?"

Oh, Lord.

No, I don't want to give it to you now.

I want *you* to give *it* to me.

Unleash that freaking Titan.

Now.

"So, where is it?" he asks.

"Oh, um, what?"

"The present. Where is it?"

"Oh, I'll go get it," I say, clearing dirty thoughts from my head, hopping off the bed, and quickly running to the closet.

I stare at the wrapped Tiffany's box sitting on the shelf,

hating myself for lying to him. I'm giving it to him now because I know I won't be there at the end of the semester.

I carry the box back to the bed and hand it to him. He leans back against the headboard and unties the white ribbon.

God, does he look sexy lying there in nothing but his underwear or what?

He smiles as he pulls out the silver keychain I bought him. It has a silver four-leaf clover charm set in a twisted circle. One side is engraved with the word *sort* and the other with the word *luck*.

"A four-leaf clover," he says with a big grin.

"Both sides of it are engraved."

He squints in the dim light, then holds the keychain in front of the hurricane lamp and reads, "*Sort*. As in the French word for fate?"

"Yeah. Now look at the other side."

He flips it over. "*Luck*. Hmmm. Luck or fate. Which one are we?"

"I don't know. But I do know I'm lucky to have met you." Tears shimmer in my eyes as he touches my face.

"I think we're both lucky."

"Remember how I told you I called you the God of all Hotties?"

He grins. "Yeah."

"That's kind of how I treated you. Like a god. Like you were perfect. But after what happened with Chelsea, seeing you with black eyes, it made you more real. And it showed me how much I care about you." I pause then say softly, "And that scared me."

"Why were you scared?"

"Because when she told me . . . " I clutch my chest, because just the thought of what she said being true still makes my heart ache.

"It hurt," Aiden says, finishing my sentence.

"Yeah."

He puts his fingers together, making half of our four-leaf clover. I hold my fingers together in the same way and touch his, forming the rest of it.

The second our fingers touch, it's like magic. A crack of thunder roars and lightening shoots across the sky as a storm moves in from the distance.

Aiden stares at me for a beat then takes action, his lips finding my neck as he quickly unbuttons the single button on his shirt and undoes my bra. He tosses them both on the bed then leans in to kiss me.

Our naked chests touch.

You sometimes hear how a teeny spark can start a whole forest fire. Our chests touching is my spark, and now I'm burning out of control.

His fingers move across my nipple, causing it to immediately harden. Then he flicks it with his tongue and pulls it into his mouth with his teeth, sending lightning bolts of sensations through my body.

My legs are spread wide, his hips between them. As he slides further down the bed, he grips my hips tightly as he kisses his way down my stomach. He kisses around the edges of my lace panties, but they aren't gentle kisses.

They're rough, harsh, ragged. And with every kiss, he pulls my hips up in a thrusting motion to meet his mouth.

I want to do something to him, but my body is consumed with what he's doing to me.

Just the anticipation of what he might do next almost sends me over the edge.

His mouth moves down farther, his tongue dancing from my thighs to my toes, causing my blood to pulse through my veins and my heart to beat wildly in one big blur of desire.

He pulls my hips toward his mouth, layering on kisses and sucking at the tender spots between my thighs. I grab ahold of his hair as I prepare for that magical tongue to move my panties aside and delve deeper.

His tongue explores the edges of the lace only, darting underneath but not staying for long.

He suddenly changes his position quickly and lies on his side next to me.

He kisses me again, his tongue thrusting into my mouth in a forceful way, almost like it's mad at me.

I reply with equal force. Coming to sit almost upright when I feel his fingers pushing aside the lace, then touching me between the soft folds.

"God, you're wet," he says, his fingers rubbing the outside of me. The friction alone is almost driving me mad.

"Oh," I moan.

But then his finger dives inside me.

Then quickly out.

And I'm lost to him.

One single finger.

One tongue.

Completely controlling my body.

Controlling my heart.

And my mind.

I arch my back. "Mhmmmm. Ohmigawd, Aiden, that feels so good."

He sucks the skin at the base of my neck while the throbbing reaches deep inside my body to places he can't touch.

After moaning an embarrassing amount, I kiss him deeply, then bravely and quickly move my hand inside his sliders and grasp the Titan.

Which, I discover, is a very appropriate name.

I should explore it but I don't.

I have but one goal.

To make him feel as good as I just did.

So I wrap my fingers around it and stroke.

Until he does.

Then we both lie flat out on the bed.

Both of us feeling completely spent.

He rolls over, pulls my back tightly into his chest, and lazily kisses my shoulder.

Just as I'm about to fall asleep—or maybe I'm already dreaming—I think I hear him whisper, *I love you.*

Friday, November 25th

ABOUT LAST NIGHT.
9AM

I WAKE UP and peek at the clock, shocked to see that it's almost nine.

I'm not ready to get up though. I want to lie in bed with Aiden all day. Revel in the glory of him. Sing praises about his chest. Write poems about his tongue. A sonnet about his lips. Buy a billboard in Times Square thanking him for his amazing fingers.

I pick his shirt up off the edge of the bed and pull it on, buttoning just the middle button.

I hug myself, loving how his shirt feels on me. And knowing that, somehow, I'm not letting it go home with him.

I lie back down and run my hand down his arm, wanting him to wake up so I can see those gorgeous green eyes.

He shifts and wraps his arm around me, pulling me close, but not speaking.

I look at the clock again.

Shit.

Fifty-two hours and counting.

"Come on, Aiden. Let's get up and get our day started. We have a lot to do."

"I thought coming to the beach meant doing nothing?" he says groggily.

"You promised to do all the stuff on my list. That starts today."

"Are we surfing this morning?"

"Maybe."

"I think we should lie here and talk about last night."

My face breaks out in a grin. "What about last night?"

"Well, for starters, you have my shirt on."

"Oh, do you want it back?"

"No. I love you naked in my shirt."

"Technically, I'm not naked if I'm wearing a shirt."

"Barely wearing," he says, touching my stomach where the shirt falls open. "This shirt is officially yours. It looks way better on you than it does on me." He studies me. "You're beautiful."

I cover my face. "I'm sure I look like a wreck."

"A beautiful wreck then. Wearing my shirt. I'd like to wake up like this every morning of my life." He gives me a naughty grin. "So back to last night."

"Why do you want to talk about it?"

"Because we finally did some of what you wanted to do. Did you like it?"

"Hmmm. Let's just say that I finally agree with what all the boys at school say about you."

"And what's that?"

"You have good hands."

Aiden laughs. "I think they were referring to my goalie skills."

I grab his hand and hold it up to mine. "You do have really big hands. And long fingers. It almost hurt."

Aiden's eyes get huge. "Did I hurt you?"

"No. God, no. Not at all. I said almost."

"Is almost good?"

"Your almost was very good."

I get the godlike smile. "It wasn't sex."

"And I'm okay with that." I start to jump up out of bed, but Aiden pulls me back down and kisses me.

THE LOVE CLIFF.
10:25AM

WE FINALLY GET out of bed, get dressed, and head to the main house for some breakfast. We find Peyton in the kitchen nursing a cup of coffee and talking animatedly with Inga.

"Where's Damian?" I ask.

"He's in the office. Business call."

"Oh, cool."

"But he said to tell you that we're going to jump off the cliff today and that you're not chickening out this time."

"You chicken out? Are you afraid of heights?" Aiden asks me as he grabs some eggs and bacon from the warming drawer.

"No, I'm not afraid of heights. I'm afraid of hitting rocks, splatting, and dying."

"Damian says that the locals call it the love cliff," Peyton informs us.

"The love cliff? That's cool," Aiden says.

"Apparently, legend says that if you hold hands and jump off the love cliff, you'll be together forever," Peyton tells us, practically cooing.

"Especially if you hit the rocks and die," I say sarcastically.

"Don't be such a cynic," Damian says, flicking my hair as he walks by.

"Funny, I've never heard it called the love cliff before," I say to Damian, who I think just totally made that whole legend up.

"It's so romantic, isn't it, though?" she asks, clasping her hands together.

"Inga, have you ever heard it called that?"

"Of course, who do you think told him about the legend?"

I roll my eyes. Okay, I can see I can't win this one. They're both liars.

"So you two in?" Damian asks, taunting me with his grin.

"It wasn't on your list," Aiden says to me. "But it sounds really fun."

"Fine. We'll go, but I'm not jumping."

WE FINISH BREAKFAST, take the Jeep, and drive across the island.

Soon, I find myself standing on a cliff looking over the edge and thinking, *No fucking way.*

"Are you sure this is a safe place to jump?" Peyton asks Damian, the romantic notion not quite as appealing when you're envisioning leaping to your death.

"Of course," he says, pulling her into his arms and murmuring something into her ear that makes her giggle.

Aiden surveys the jump. "So you've been up here before?"

"Yes."

"And you've seen people jump and survive?"

"Yes."

"But you've never done it before?"

"No. What's with the twenty questions? I said I'd come, but I'm not jumping. Please don't try to talk me into it."

He kisses my cheek. "I'm doing it. I want you to jump with me. Off the love cliff."

I roll my eyes. "Aiden, I'll cheer you on. Besides, someone has to be here to scrape you guys off the rocks and take your bodies home."

He tickles my sides. "You're being silly."

"I know. It's scary though."

"It is really high. It's gonna be a rush."

"We're going for it!" Damian yells. He grabs Peyton's hand, kisses it, and then they run and jump, both of them screaming all the way down.

I look over the edge and see them pop up out of the water.

"They're alive!" Aiden says, mocking me.

"Watch it, or I might just push you off."

"You just saw Damian and Peyton do it and survive."

"I know."

Just as he's about to reply, the breeze blows grass and leaves around us in a little circle.

"Did you see the movie *Pocahontas*?" he asks.

"Yeah."

"That breeze was like the colors of the wind. The earth is telling you to jump with me."

"Oh, really?"

"Yeah, don't you remember how she jumped off the waterfall? This is nothing compared to that. Just a little old cliff."

I shake my head no.

"Hmm," he says, pulling me into his arms. "The Disney

references didn't work. Guess I'm gonna have to pull out the big guns."

"What big guns?"

He touches my face gently, looks into my soul, and says, "Do you trust me?"

I close my eyes and for the first time since Vincent tried to kidnap me, I listen to my heart. "Yes."

He kisses me then whispers, "Then jump with me."

I start to get tears in my eyes. I know this is just a stupid jump, but it feels like so much more.

I nod.

He turns and faces the edge, grabs my hand tightly, and says, "Run!"

I scream as we flail through the air and drop for what seems like both forever and an instant.

When we hit the water, I open my eyes and swim to the surface.

For a second, I can't find Aiden.

Panic spreads through me. Where is he? Did he hit his head? Did he not come up?

I frantically scan the surface of the water trying to find any sign of him. Then I spin around to find him just behind me.

"We made it," he says, pulling me close and kissing me. "What a freaking rush!"

"What the hell is that?" Damian says.

"What's what?"

Damian points at us. I look down in the water and see bubbles all around us.

"What the hell?" Aiden says too, scooping up a handful and examining them.

I start laughing.

"What's so funny?" Aiden asks.

"I . . . have . . . bubbles . . ." I manage to choke out between laughs.

"Like, bubble bath?" Peyton says, trying to understand.

"Yeah, we took a bubble bath at my loft, and Aiden had that swimsuit on."

"You took a bubble bath wearing a swimsuit?" Damian laughs. "There's something just wrong with that."

But Aiden and I don't care. We can't stop laughing.

Or kissing.

WE MAKE THE long hike back to the top of the cliff, then drive to the nearest town, have fried fish at a shack on the beach, and head back to the house.

TOTALLY DID THE DEED.
2PM

DAMIAN AND I are lying in the sun while Peyton and Aiden are inside talking to their parents on the phone.

Damian squints at me. "You two are awfully tight today. You totally did the deed last night."

I shake my head at him. "No," I say, like the deed is the grossest thing ever.

"Something happened."

I blush and look completely guilty.

"Tell me what happened," he demands.

"Um, well, I touched it."

"You touched what?"

"*It.* You know, his boy part."

Damian snickers. "Seriously, Keats, you shouldn't be touching it if you aren't mature enough to say it. Besides, what's the big deal?"

"Shut up. And it's a big deal for us. I mean, I still haven't actually seen it, but I kinda felt it."

"Felt it, or did something to it?"

"Fine. I did something to it with my hand."

"That would be called a hand job, Keats. Say it with me now. H-a-n-d J-o-b."

I smack him. "I can say hand job. I just didn't really want to. At least not in reference to Aiden."

"He's spent the weekend at your loft. He's sleeping in your bed. Have you gotten naked with him?"

"Speaking of naked. I saw you and Peyton skinny-dipping last night."

"Oh, that was fun. You should try it. And why haven't you been naked? What are you waiting for?"

"You know why, Damian. Because it will just make it harder to say goodbye."

He glances at Aiden, who's beaming as he walks out of the great room doors, making his way down to the beach, spiked tropical smoothies in hand.

"The way he's been grinning and all over you, I totally thought you guys fu—"

I cover my ears. "Don't say it. Oh, God, I shouldn't have touched it, should I? I'm totally leading him on. Fuck. Fuck. Fuck."

"Now that sounds like more fun."

"So, does the fact that you're following Peyton around like she's a piece of steak mean you haven't yet?"

"I don't want her to think this is just a hookup, so I'm trying to be good. But, damn, if she doesn't have the most amazing mouth."

"Like for kissing, you mean?"

Damian coughs. "For kissing something."

"Oh. God. No. I don't need that visual, please. You showed me yours when we were twelve and I still haven't fully recovered."

"It was so massive it scared you?"

"No, it was a disgusting limp-looking little thing. And I couldn't possibly fathom how sex actually worked."

Damian smiles. "So then I showed you that magazine."

I cover my face with my hands. "Please make him stop," I say to Aiden, who joins us, holding my drink out in front of me.

"Stop what?"

Damian smirks. "Why don't you tell him what we were discussing, Keats? Peyton and I are going to kayak for a bit."

When Peyton walks out of the house, Damian jumps up, kisses her in greeting, then grabs her hand and pulls her toward the boat.

Aiden puts his smoothie glass against mine. "This is really good. So, what were you talking about?"

"Seeing a, um, penis for the first time."

"Is it an embarrassing story?"

"No, I just . . . it's just hard to comprehend the mechanics of sex when you're young and you see it in its, um, natural state."

"Natural state? Like, out in the wild?"

"No, not in the wild. I saw a boy's"—I wave my hand slowly across my body—"in its natural state."

"As opposed to its *unnatural* state?"

"Its, um, softer state," I finally say, trying not to think about how his felt in my hand. How I wanted to rip those sliders off his body. Touch it. Feel it. Taste it.

He leans in. "You're thinking about last night right now, aren't you?"

I feel my cheeks turn red. Why am I such a prude about

sex when it comes to Aiden? You'd think I'd never done it before. "I, uh . . ."

Aiden arches an eyebrow at me. "Maybe tonight you can see it in its, uh, unnatural state," he says with a laugh as he kisses my cheek. "You're adorable. What's next on our list?"

"Swim with the dolphins. But that's not going to happen."

"Yeah, it is. We're lucky when we're together."

"We're not allowed to take the wave runners out if we're drinking, but since we're just going straight out there"—I point straight ahead of me—"and sitting, it will be okay. Are you sure you won't be bored?"

"I'm never bored when I'm with you."

"Don't say I didn't warn you," I laugh, grabbing my drink and heading to the dock. I get the wave runner lowered off the dock and Aiden jumps on the seat behind me. I drive us straight out from the house where the water is deeper and turn off the engine. "So, we'll just sit here and wait. The waves will float us back toward the shore, so if we haven't seen any by that time, we'll give up. Deal?"

"That's fine with me," he says, grabbing my waist, pulling me onto his lap, and kissing the back of my neck. "I'll just do this. You can be on lookout." He moves my ponytail off to one side and continues kissing my neck while his hands move up my stomach to caress my bikini top.

When his hand slides under my top, I laugh and say, "You're going to scare them away."

"Turn around so I can kiss you," he tells me. Then he laughs. "Maybe I should untie these strings and toss your top in the water. I bet all the boy dolphins will come running."

"I don't think dolphins can run," I reply teasingly as I stand up carefully then turn around and sit on his lap.

He immediately kisses me, muttering, "Much better," into my lips.

Our kissing gets deeper, more intense, and I forget where I am and why I'm out here.

All I can focus on is his lips.

His tongue.

His hands roaming across my body.

The way my fingers feel in his hair. Across his back.

I grind myself into his lap with every kiss. With every suck.

My mind on one thing and one thing only.

All of a sudden, we get splashed.

I open my eyes quickly, worried that a boat came too close to us, but there are no boats around.

Then I hear a chirping noise behind me and a dolphin jumps up out of the water and does a flip, splashing us with water again.

"Oh my gosh!" I whisper to Aiden. "Did you just see that?"

"I think he's showing off for you," Aiden says. "He better not be trying to steal my girl."

My breath catches, my stomach getting instant butter-flies, and my heart soaring. Because, *his* girl?

"Look," he whispers, "there's three more, right there."

"And two more over here," I whisper back.

"Don't move," he says, hugging me tighter.

"I've never been this close to one before."

"Are you going to swim with them?"

"Oh, no. You're not supposed to actually swim with wild dolphins. This is what I meant. Like being out here, seeing them, feeling like I'm part of it."

One of the dolphins flies high out of the water with another one following him.

"It's like they're playing tag," Aiden whispers, still holding me tightly on his lap. "They're huge."

We watch with wonder as they swim and play around us, but just as quickly as they came, they're gone, swimming off into the distance.

My arms are still wrapped around Aiden's neck, so I pull his adorable face closer to me. "You're right. We are lucky together."

We kiss a bit.

Okay, we kiss a lot.

Damian was right. Since last night, I can't keep my hands—or my lips—off him. I've even stopped counting down the hours until he leaves. I'm just going to enjoy this.

Aiden pushes the pieces of my bangs that have fallen out of my ponytail and are blowing in the wind off my face, tucking them behind my ear.

"That was amazing."

"You're amazing, Aiden."

He rubs his thumb across my cheek.

It's a perfect moment.

Soft breeze, brilliant sun warm on our skin, beautiful scenery.

Every part of me wants to tell him. To say it out loud.

And, most of all, for him to know.

But I can't.

I can't do that to him.

So I say *I love you, Aiden* in my head.

"So, what's next on the list?" he asks.

"Um, write our names in the sand, maybe. And we definitely need to look for seashells."

"Sounds like a plan," he says as I flip around, start the wave runner, and head back to shore.

WHEN WE GET there, Damian waves at us from the beach, indicating that he wants me to bring it up on shore.

"Hey," he says, walking out in the water. "The other wave runner won't start. If you're done with this one, I'm gonna take Peyton out and show her some of the island from the water."

"Yeah, we're done," I say as Aiden and I hop off. "Did you see the dolphins that were swimming all around us?"

"No, we were, uh, in the house."

"I thought you were kayaking?" Aiden asks.

"Oh, we were, but we came back in as soon as you went out."

"So what were you doing inside?" Aiden asks them.

"Uh, relaxing," Damian answers as Peyton says, "Watching TV."

Aiden squints his eyes. "Which one was it?"

"I watched TV while he relaxed," Peyton says smoothly.

Aiden grabs her by the elbow and pulls her aside. I'm pretty sure he's chewing her out and she's telling him to mind his own business.

She marches away from him and pulls Damian out toward the water.

Aiden's scowling toward them, so I walk up to him and say, "She's having fun."

"She's acting like she loves him already. They just freaking met."

"She told me it was love at first sight."

Aiden nods. "She told me that too."

"And do you believe in it?"

"Yes, of course I do."

"Then you understand why she needs to see it through."

Aiden nods solemnly then grabs my hand. "Come on, we have some things to do."

"Like what?"

He runs down the beach, dragging me with him, through the water, the waves spraying water up on us.

Then he stops, grabs me around the waist, lifts me off my feet, and kisses me.

And kisses me.

I feel like I'm starring in an amazing beach-set love story.

I don't want this day to ever end.

"This looks like the perfect spot," Aiden says, setting me down in the sand, but not letting me go. "Remember that bracelet you had on the day of the Gods of the Olympics competition? You had love written on your arm."

"I remember."

"Close your eyes and don't move."

A FEW MOMENTS later, he comes up from behind me, wraps his arms around my waist, and whispers, "Open."

I open my eyes and look at the sand in front of me.

"Love in the sand," he says. "I put it higher on the beach so the water wouldn't wash it away."

I want to cry. "The water always washes it away," I tell him.

"Maybe the words, but not the feelings." He spins me out of his arms in a dance move and says, "Go write your name."

I move a little ways down the beach, fighting back tears, and wondering if he could be right.

I find a stick and use it to draw all sorts of doodles in the sand. Hearts, flowers, swirls, a castle, a frog, a wand, lips, stars, a moon, a rock, waves, a surfboard, the chaos symbol, fireworks, a soccer ball, pompoms, a four-leaf clover, and then, in big, bold, capital letters, *KEATYN.*

Aiden says, "I wish I had my phone to take a picture. That's, like, a work of art." He studies it more closely. "Is that the story of your life?"

"What?"

"Oh, it just looks like you drew all the things you love."

I study my sand doodles more closely, realizing he might be right. I smile at him. "I was just messing around, drawing random things, but they are all things I love."

He points over at his name written in the sand. Just a simple *Aiden*. "Mine looks pretty lame in comparison."

"Actually, yours looks perfect," I tell him, wrapping my arms around his neck. "It says everything about you."

"That I'm boring?"

"No, that you don't need any embellishments to make you stand out. You just do."

He gives me a hug and kisses my forehead. "I saw some shells down here by the waterline. Want to gather some up?"

"Yeah, let's do that and then we'll go make necklaces!"

We gather shells, filling his board shorts' pockets with them.

When we get closer to the cabana, I stick my tongue out, splash him, and then run down the beach screaming, "Bet you can't catch me!"

Of course, I'm not as fast as him and two seconds later, he grabs me from behind.

I deftly spin out of his grip, kick water at him, then land in a karate stance, and go, "Ka-cha!"

"Oh, you're gonna fight me?" he says with a laugh.

"Unless you're a chicken," I reply, kicking more water at him.

He makes one fluid leap and tackles me straight into the water.

I was totally not prepared for it and come up laughing.

"What the hell was that? That wasn't even fair!"

He rolls me over and pins me on the sand underneath him. "Maybe I'm tired of playing fair."

I lean up like I'm going to kiss him, but instead elbow him in the ribs and slip away.

Almost.

He grabs my legs, pulls me back underneath him, and pins my arms above my head.

Truth be told, I totally could've gotten away if I wanted to. I've learned a lot from Cooper. But when he leans down to kiss me, I'm really glad I didn't.

The waves rush up over our feet and legs, the cool water doing nothing to quench the fire inside me. I don't even care that my hair is probably getting caked with wet, nasty sand.

Because when Aiden kisses me, I don't care what the rest of the world thinks.

A DING-DONG DITCHER.
7:30PM

WE COLLECT SOME more shells, watch the sun slide below the horizon, and then sort through our shells, deciding which ones will work best for our shell jewelry.

"Come on. We'll go in the toy shed to make them. There're power tools in there."

"Hammers, nails, and screws?"

"Yes, they do have those things, but to make the jewelry we'll use a drill."

"Drilling sounds like fun," he says with a naughty smirk.

As I clean the shells off with bleach, I say, "You know, you've become a tease."

"I'm a tease?" he asks, pointing to himself.

"Yeah, you're a ding-dong ditcher."

"I don't get it."

"Think about it. You act like you want in my house. You keep ringing the doorbell, but when I come to open the door, you're gone. You're totally a tease."

He puts his forehead against mine. "I told you I won't run away."

"Honestly, Aiden, if you were smart," I say, seriously, "you'd run far away from me."

He tenderly touches my cheek. "My dad says love makes you do stupid things."

I want so badly to say, *Love?* And for him to answer, *Yes, Boots, I love you.* But I can't bear to hear it, so I let out a nervous chuckle. "That's true. I think all of us have done some pretty stupid things in the name of love. So, back to these shells," I say, patting them dry. "Next, we'll drill them. Here are the little shells we picked for you. Do you want to have a single shell or a whole row of them?"

He slides the most perfect teeny pink seashell out of the pile and touches my four-leaf clover necklace. "Can I have this?"

He doesn't wait for an answer; he reaches his arms around my neck and unclasps it.

He lays the shell on a piece of felt, drills a hole in the top of it, adds a little metal circle to turn it into a charm, and then slides it onto my necklace with the clover charm.

He puts it back on me, and I look in the mirror. The clover nestles perfectly on top of the shell.

I hold the charms in my hand. "I love it."

"You know, they say the moon controls the tides. So now you'll have both luck and the tides of fate on your side."

I smile at him as he pushes me up against the work-bench and flirts. "Which means you're about to get very lucky."

His lips land hard on mine, his tongue sliding into my mouth, and controlling the tides of desire that roll through my body.

"Uh, um," Damian coughs, interrupting our hot make-out session.

"Oh, hey," I say, untangling myself from Aiden. "Uh, we were, um, just making jewelry."

"I can see that," Damian smirks. "We got a bunch of shells too."

"Awesome!" I turn my attention back to the shells, but Aiden's hand is still on my back, touching both my skin and the top of my bikini bottoms. And although I am trying to sort through shells to make him the perfect wish bracelet, I'm having a really hard time concentrating.

Especially when he starts massaging my back gently.

I choose shells and then drill holes on the sides of each, sliding them onto a string one at a time and putting a square knot in between each. "Where do you want it?"

Aiden's eyes get big and he gulps. "Uh . . . ?"

I realize very quickly what he was just thinking. "Your ankle or your wrist?" I add.

He does a little head shake, like he's clearing out the cobwebs in his brain. "My wrist. So I can see it."

"Okay." I lay the shells across the top of his wrist. "This is a wish bracelet. As I tie it on, you have to close your eyes and make a wish."

"Then what? When do I get my wish?"

"We don't know when, but once you get your wish, the bracelet will fall off."

He gives Peyton and Damian, who are sorting through

and washing off shells a glance, then he whispers sexily, "Can I wish for drilling?"

"You can wish for whatever you want."

"So I'll be losing the bracelet tonight?"

I try to control my smile, but I can't.

Because Aiden the tease is the cutest thing ever.

I roll my eyes at him and smack his hand away from where it's sneaking down the side of my bikini.

Plus it's so much more fun to be the one to say no.

"This wish business is serious," I tell him as I tie the bracelet around his wrist, purposefully tying it in three tight knots. Maybe if I tie it tight enough, he won't be able to get it off.

And maybe he won't forget me when I'm gone.

I picture Aiden back at Eastbrooke, surrounded by girls at the Cave, and quickly close my eyes to keep from crying.

"Are you wishing on my bracelet too?" he asks.

Part of me wants to curse his bracelet, so that no one else's lips will ever touch his.

But I know I'm being ridiculous. I'm giving him closure so that he can move on.

"No," I say, fighting back tears.

"Why do you look like you're about to cry?"

"I'm not. I think I got shell dust in my eyes." I wipe tears from the corner of my eyes. "I was supposed to wear safety goggles when I drilled."

"You need safety goggles for drilling?" he says, grabbing a pair. "Maybe I should bring a pair to bed."

I grab his now shell-wrapped wrist. "Come on, we've got to finish our list."

I DRAG HIM to a hammock that's strung between two palm trees in the courtyard between two of the guest suites.

"Lie in the hammock and read? There's only one problem. We don't have any books."

"We don't need a book. We have some homework to do."

He groans. "You're going to make me study French?"

"No, but it turns out that I have this survey I have to do for health class."

"You're not in health class."

"Neither are you. I had to answer your questions, now you have to answer mine."

He rolls his eyes and pulls me closer to his chest. "Fine. I'm an open book."

"Names of the last four girls you dated."

"Emily, Lauren, Megan, and Chelsea."

"Why did you break up?"

"Um, Emily and I got in a fight about something stupid. I honestly don't remember. She was always accusing me of cheating on her."

"Were you?"

He looks at me seriously. "I've never cheated on anyone in my life."

"Good."

"What about the rest?"

"Lauren broke up with me because she decided she liked someone else. Megan and I had a very volatile relationship. That was a mutual break up. And Chelsea. Um, we never actually went out."

"How many girls have you said I love you to?"

"Oh, the list is long. The first girl was Angela; she stole my heart in third grade when she gave me a special Valentine's card. She was a fourth grader. Older woman, you know."

"Maybe we don't need to go back quite so far," I laugh.

"And I'm ready for dinner and some wine. Where do you want to eat?"

"Can we watch a movie while we eat?"

"That sounds fun. Then what?"

"Then, Miss Monroe, we're going dancing."

SCREAMING A LOT.
8:30PM

WE SET OURSELVES up in back of the theater room at the bar table, deciding to watch a little college football while we eat. We enjoy part of the game, our dinner, and the whole bottle of wine.

"I'll go grab another bottle," I tell him. "You pick out a movie."

When I come back with the bottle, he holds up a couple movies. "I've narrowed it down to two. Which was really tough considering all the options."

"They do have a lot of movies," I say, moving our glasses and the wine cooler up to the theater seats in the front. "What'd you come up with?"

"Well, since we're on an island, I went with a water theme. So we have *Jaws*, which may be a bad idea, since we'll be out surfing again in the morning, or *A Day at the Lake*, which I've never gotten to see but is one of my parents' favorites."

I freeze in the middle of pouring more wine when he mentions my mom's movie. The movie that Vincent wants to remake. The movie that started all this.

I've seen the movie before. A few years ago. But I don't really remember all that much of it, and I don't know why I didn't think of it before. I need to study this movie. I need to understand the script. I need to try to figure out what Vincent has in mind.

"*A Day at the Lake,*" I say, sounding too eager. "I mean, I definitely don't want to have bad dreams about being attacked by a shark."

"Have you ever seen it before?" he asks me.

"A few years ago, I kinda watched it on TV. But it was one of those things where it was on, but I wasn't really watching. So I've never seen the whole thing. I just remember the girl in the bikini screaming a lot."

"Perfect," he says. "We'll watch it and then go dancing."

I snuggle up on the big padded couch next to him, sip my wine, and press play.

The movie starts out showing my mom's character in her everyday world. Hanging out with her hot frat boyfriend. Her friends hanging out and planning their weekend party at the lake. Figuring out how to get all the alcohol they needed. Who is bringing the weed. The guys are looking forward to hooking up. The girls want to work on their tans. Mom and her boyfriend are adorable together, say they love each other, and have a couple romantic scenes. But there's also a scene where they argue about an archeology semester abroad she really wants to do. You get the impression that he's not supportive of her dreams, so you're not really sure what to think about their relationship as they head to the lake.

We watch, drink more wine, and then Aiden starts kissing me.

Saturday, November 26th

A DANGEROUS JOURNEY.
9AM

I WAKE UP, wondering where I am.

I squint my eyes, seeing only darkness and feeling Aiden's arm across my shoulder. I remember that we were in the theater room, watching Mom's movie, drinking wine, and kissing.

We must've both fallen asleep.

Aiden is still breathing heavily, and I sadly realize that I'm down to my last twenty-four hours with him. That it's our last night together.

Tick. Tick. Tick.

I get up and go find Inga. I need to see if she'll make us a special dinner tonight. We'll watch the sunset from the beach, have an amazing meal in the moonlight, and then I'll tell him that I'm not going back.

The moonlight.

I suppose that will be a fitting place to tell him I'm leaving, since it's the damn moon's fault. It's like rubbing a dog's nose down by where they peed on the carpet.

I want the moon to see what it did.

I shake my head. It sucks. But I have to do it.

"Inga, since it's our last night here, I'd like to do a special dinner on the beach at sunset. Would that be possible?"

"Of course. What would you like on the menu? I have some filets and some fresh mahi-mahi."

"That sounds yummy. Could we have a little of both?"

"Absolutely." She glances around her kitchen and then grabs my palm. "May I have a closer look?"

"Um, sure."

She looks at one palm and then studies the other, shaking her head. "I had a dream about you last night."

"You did?"

"Well, about your palm. I dreamed that the line, here, moved. And now I look at it and see that it was not just a dream, but more of a prophecy." She shakes her head at me. "I've never had something like that happen before."

"What do you mean?"

She holds up my left hand. "This hand is what could be." Then she holds up my right hand. "This hand is what is. This line. The one running through your life line on your right hand was not clear before."

"Does that, like, mean something important?"

She nods solemnly. "This line breaks your life line. Remember this one, up here, where I said you had cheated death?"

I swallow hard. "Um, yes."

"I believe death is coming back for you."

"Oh," I say.

She stares at me. "You're not surprised by this. You are about to embark on a dangerous journey, yes?"

I can't do anything but nod in agreement.

"And you know that you may not survive?"

I nod again. "Yes."

She wipes her reading glasses off on her apron, puts them back on, and studies my palm some more. "Maybe you should consider canceling this journey?"

I shake my head. "I can't. It's something I have to do."

"It is about getting your life back?"

I nod again.

"You love him, yes?"

"Yes."

"Inga will cook you an amazing dinner."

I nod and give her a grateful smile. "Thank you."

I WALK TO the great room window and look out at the ocean, so many thoughts going through my head, when Aiden leans his chin on my shoulder.

"You ditched me."

"I was coming back for you."

"You better always come back for me."

I reach down and grasp his hand, giving it a squeeze and praying that will even be an option.

"So what's on tap for today? We haven't done yoga in the sand yet. Or built a sand village."

"We're surfing and snorkeling today," I hear Damian say.

"And going to get tattoos," Peyton adds.

"Tattoos, really?" Aiden says excitedly. "I've been wanting a tattoo."

"Really? What do you want?"

He grins at me. "I want a four-leaf clover, right here." He flips my hand over and shows me a spot on his wrist.

"That's cool. What about you, Damian?"

"I'm getting the tribal tattoo I've always wanted around my bicep. So grab some food and let's get out there. Did you see the waves this morning, Keats? They're the best since we've been here."

"Awesome," I say, happy for something to keep my mind off the inevitable.

WE SURF AND build a sand village, but decided to skip yoga and go snorkeling instead.

"Everyone be sure to put lots of sunblock on before we leave," I tell everyone when we're in the toy shed getting flippers and snorkel masks.

Aiden grabs a can of sunblock and sprays our backs.

We swim out a ways and enjoy all the cool marine life for a couple hours.

Then we head back in for lunch.

IN THE KITCHEN, I notice Aiden's back. "Oh, your back is pretty sunburned."

"Yeah, it feels hot. I sprayed everyone else's but forgot to do my own."

"I'm sorry," I tell him, giving him gentle hug.

He wraps me up tighter. "It doesn't hurt that bad."

We all sit down, eat, and talk.

"The fish were so amazing!" Peyton says excitedly. "So many cool colors!"

"I loved the turtles we saw."

"They were pretty cool, but I think those blue fish with the little yellow spots were my favorite," Aiden says.

"I saw a shark," Damian says coolly, "but I didn't wanna freak you all out."

We all laugh, knowing that Damian is teasing us.

"I'm thinking about getting a shark tattoo, as a matter of fact."

"No, you're not," I say. "You've never wanted a shark tattoo until just now. If you're going to get a tattoo, it should mean something to you."

"Yeah, like the band I'm getting means I'm a badass."

"And my clover will bring me even more luck. You should get one too."

"I already have a tattoo. What are you getting, Peyton?"

"I'm getting a butterfly. They symbolize transformation and this last week has sort of changed my life. You know, all that went on at school, what I've realized, and then coming here. I feel new and happy."

"That's amazing," I tell her as Damian snuggles with her.

AFTER LUNCH, DAMIAN says, "Okay, everyone get cleaned up and then we'll head into town for tattoos!"

"I'm gonna go take a shower," Aiden tells me.

"Okay, I'm gonna help Inga clean up and then I'll be over to get ready too."

Everyone leaves and Inga says, "I saw that boy's back." She drops a bag in my lap. "Here, this is aloe vera soap and some lotion. I want you to go over there while he's in the shower and very carefully wash his back with this soap. Then gently pat the area dry and put a thin layer of lotion on it."

I'm thinking about Aiden being naked in the shower and how I'm supposed to accomplish all this when she says, "Shoo."

HIS OFFICIAL TITLE.
2PM

I GET TO my room and peek around the corner at the glass shower.

The shower glass is starting to fog over, but I can see his naked outline.

I look at the soap in my hand and imagine sudsing up Aiden's entire body.

All of it.

I wonder if I should get naked?

Stop it. This is not about seduction. The poor man is probably in pain, and I'm here in a purely professional capacity.

I leave my swimsuit on, grab a washcloth off the towel rack, and open the shower door.

His back is turned to me.

And what a back it is.

His body looks like it is carved out of stone. The study of the perfect male form.

And his ass.

Oh my god. His naked, beautiful ass.

I'm reaching out to touch it when he turns around.

"Boots!" he says startled, automatically covering his private parts, but pulling me under the water with him and close enough to him so that I can't see what I was hoping to see. "I'm glad you decided to join me."

"I didn't. Um, I brought you aloe soap for your back. Inga gave it to me. Told me it would help with your burn."

"So you didn't just want to see me naked?"

I squint my eyes at him. "This is my bathroom. You shouldn't be taking a shower in here if you didn't want to be seen naked. You were totally hoping I'd come in and catch a glimpse." I hand him the washcloth. "Here, I even brought this so you can cover yourself up."

He takes the washcloth, looks at it, and laughs. "It's not big enough," he says, but he still covers up with it. Then he looks down my bikini top and shakes his head. "That's what

I was afraid of."

"What?"

"You have a severe case of reverse sunburn. See this part under your top? It didn't get the sun that it needed. It's white and needs this soap rubbed on it," he says as he unties the strings of my bikini top, allowing it to fall to the tile.

He takes the soap out of my hand and washes my chest very slowly then he moves us in front of a sprayer to rinse the soap off before replacing the soap with his lips.

I'm trying to be good. I'm trying not to reach down and grab the washcloth. Rip it off of him.

But it's like the Titan is calling out to me.

And it's like I now have two Keatyns sitting on my shoulders. Good angel Keatyn is telling me not to do it. The horned and horny bad Keatyn is telling me that I need to do a whole lot more than touch it.

Good Keatyn screams, *No! You can't sleep with a boy you're going to say goodbye to.*

Bad Keatyn says, *And that's exactly why we should sleep with him. We may never get another chance.*

Aiden drops the soap, so I bend down to pick it up.

As I start to stand back up, I see it.

The Titan is fully erect, but mostly hidden under the washcloth. But the washcloth is wet, molding itself to it and allowing me to see its full outline.

My insides throb just seeing it.

I also realize that I was very stupid to give him one of the Morans' thick white washcloths. I totally should have given him a tissue.

But, still, something about the white cloth covering it looks very godlike. I halfway wish I had a little mini gold wreath to crown it with.

Lord Titan, God of the Underworld.

God of Hammering, Nailing, and Screwing.

Yes. This is his official title.

I imagine my body as a homecoming float. Aiden using his godly tool on me.

I drop the soap, wrap my arms around his neck and kiss him hard.

We kiss wildly. Passionately. Like people starved for each other.

"Do you want me to take these off?" he asks, tugging on my bottoms.

I shake my head no as I run one of my hands across my chest, good Keatyn's way of reminding me about my heart.

Aiden watches me intently, then backs away slightly. "God, that's hot."

"What's hot?"

"What you just did. Rubbing yourself. Do it again."

I tilt my head back, close my eyes, and run the tips of my fingers from the base of my neck slowly down toward my cleavage and then down my stomach. Aiden moves so that he is standing behind me. He kisses my neck, then lays his hand on top of mine and guides it where he wants it to go.

Up to my boob, then slowly running circles around my nipple.

Up the side of my neck to where his lips are, our hands moving together from my neck to his stubbled cheek.

Then he guides my hand in a slow descent straight down to the throbbing spot between my legs. He pushes our fingers against the fabric of my bikini bottoms while he sucks on my neck.

The feel of his mouth on my neck, the water drizzling down my skin, and his hand between my legs makes me feel perfectly out of control.

He keeps kissing me and rubbing our hands with more intensity.

Wanting to maintain some level of attractiveness, I try to make cute, sweet little noises. They start out that way, until I don't give a shit what I sound like.

I move my hips in rhythm with our hands until I can't hold it in any longer. A deep *oh* leaves my lips as my body trembles and throbs and my legs start to feel weak.

Aiden growls something unintelligible in my ear, picks me up, and sets me on a tiled ledge that I thought was for shampoo, but now realize is the perfect height for this.

I wrap my legs around his waist as his lips land hard on mine, his tongue delving deeply in my mouth.

"I'm not telling you no again," he says.

I so want him to rip my bottoms to shreds and plunge that beast inside of me, but that will just make tomorrow even harder.

Speaking of hard.

He pushes the Titan forcefully against my bottoms, which are straining to keep it out.

I kiss down his neck and then find his hungry lips again.

I can tell that he's struggling not to lose control, but I want him to.

I want to be the one who makes him feel out of control.

Plus, I'm on the edge again. Wanting the release, but not wanting it to be over.

I lean my back against the wall, grab his butt tightly, and push back against him.

Then, eventually, we both lose control.

HE LEANS AGAINST me, keeping me pinned against the wall, and breathes deeply.

"See, we can have lots of fun without actually doing it,"

I say as he sets me down on wobbly legs.

He doesn't really reply, just pulls my bikini bottoms slowly off me, rinses them out, lays them on the ledge to dry, and wraps a towel around me while he kisses me.

"You continue to surprise me," he says, while we're drying off.

"Why?"

"All you had to do was slide your bottoms over a fraction of an inch."

"I know. I just . . . I mean . . . Maybe we can just play in the backyard for awhile."

He cocks an eyebrow at me. "You like it in the backyard?"

"I'm talking the *backyard* not the back door."

"I'm confused," he says.

"You know, like playing in the backyard as opposed to playing inside the house."

He gives me a naughty grin. "So eventually you will want me to play in the *interior* portion of your house?"

"Aiden, I've wanted to have sex with you since I met you. But when you got mad at me for trying to unzip your pants, I wasn't going to invite you in. I just wanted to have some fun playing outside."

"So I was at least right about you wanting to wait?"

"Yes. I do want to wait."

"Until when?"

"Until I know we have a chance," I say softly, meaning not until I get my life back.

THE GREEN FLASH.
4:30PM

AFTER GOING TO town, getting tattoos, and coming back home, I tell Aiden I want to get ready in my room alone, but ask him to meet me at my door at 5:20.

"Five-twenty?" he says, kissing my nose. "That's very specific."

"There's a reason why it's very specific, but it's a surprise."

He leans on my doorframe, looking like he has no intention of letting me get ready by myself. "I'm glad you got the tattoo," he says, flipping my wrist over and looking at the four-leaf clover on it.

He says it in a dreamy way that makes me feel guilty. I'm afraid he thinks I got it just because of him. What he doesn't know is that it's about so much more.

"I like it too. I'm glad you talked me into it. Now you have to go."

"I want to watch you get ready," he says. And the way he says it touches my heart. It's like somehow he instinctively knows this is our last night together.

"Please, Aiden. I haven't really fixed my hair or done my makeup all week and I want to look nice on our last night here."

He kisses me and says, "Your wish is my command."

I GET READY, doing my hair up in big curls, teasing the crown a little, and applying more eye makeup than normal. I even added a glittery gold powder across the tops of my lids that I hope will glimmer in the moonlight.

At 5:20 on the dot, Aiden knocks on my door.

As soon as I open the door, he takes in my dramatic

shimmering orange silk ruffled dress and says, "Wow. You look gorgeous."

"Thanks, but come on. We have to hurry," I say, dragging him down to the beach.

I watch his face as he sees the table set up for two in the sand, tiki torches blazing around it.

"Is all this for us?"

"Yes, we're going to have some wine, watch the sunset, and then have dinner here in the moonlight."

"We are supposed to watch a million sunsets together," he says adorably.

I look at the sun moving down the horizon and listen to the waves crash.

I have to tell him tonight.

Just not now.

I pour us each a glass of wine and ask, "Have you ever seen the green flash?"

"Like the super hero?"

"No, like, just as the sun goes down, right before you can't see it anymore, sometimes, if you watch carefully, you can see a green flash. Some people say it's a myth. I just think it's magical."

"So have you seen it before?"

"Yeah, but not everyone sees it."

"We'll both see it tonight."

"You're always so sure of everything."

"Only the things that have to do with us."

We toast to sunsets and sit and watch the sun move closer and closer to the ocean.

"Look," he says, pointing toward the horizon, "I think it's almost time."

He grabs my hand. And when he squeezes it, all of a sudden, I see it.

The green flash.

"Oh my gosh!" I yell.

"Did you see it too?" Aiden asks excitedly. "Was that it? I've never seen anything like that before. The sun literally turned green for a second. How did it do that?"

"Yes, I saw it! But I've never seen it do that before! It was amazing!"

"But you told me that you had seen it before."

"I think I lied."

He cocks his eyebrow at me.

"Not on purpose. I think I've wanted to see it so bad that I thought I had. But I didn't know I hadn't really seen it until I just saw the real thing."

Aiden reaches out and touches my cheek. "Kinda like the difference between loves."

"The sunset was like loves?"

"Yeah, like, everyone falls in love at different times in their lives. And when you're in it, you think you know what it's like to be in love. Until you meet your true love and then you know the other love wasn't the same thing."

I nod at him, understanding what he's saying.

He grabs his phone out of his pocket, presses a few buttons, and reads, "It's an optical phenomenon caused by the refraction of light . . ."

I take the phone out of his hand. "Don't read that, Aiden. I don't want to know if there's a scientific reason for it. I don't want to take the magic out of it," I say as I walk over to a fake rock just above the sand line, pop it open, and connect his phone to the beach's speaker system, turning on our twenty-nine song playlist.

"May I have this dance?"

"Yes."

He pulls me into his arms and sways with me.

"You were pretty hot in the shower," I tell him.

"And you wore the skimpiest bikini known to man today. No wonder I can barely control myself."

"I did not. It's not like I had on a thong. No one needs to see my naked ass."

"I do," he says with a grin as he twirls and then dips me.

"Dinner is served," Sven tells us, setting our dinner on the table.

THIS ONE'S FOR YOU.
10:30PM

WE'RE ALL IN the hot tub, being careful to keep our tattoos out of the water and listening to Damian entertain us with stories from his recent tour of Japan. About how he couldn't fit his knees under the table at a fast food restaurant because the table was so small. About the ongoing pranks the band plays on each other. And even what's up next for him.

Peyton talks about school and the things she's looking forward to. How she's thinking about graduating early. About how she's not ready to go back.

Aiden tells us a few funny family stories and I tell a couple about my crazy little sisters.

Damian says, "I think we need some champagne," just as Sven walks out onto the pool deck.

"There's a call for you on the house phone, Mr. Damian," he says, handing him a handset.

Damian puts the phone up to his ear, gets a huge grin on his face, puts the phone on speaker, and says, "Holy shit, you've got to hear this, Keats."

I squint my eyes, like it will help me hear better, and

lean toward the phone.

There's all sorts of noise. Almost like it's a concert. Is this *Twisted Dreams* playing at the Undertow without him?

But then I hear B's voice yell, "You guys are never gonna believe this. Hell, I can barely believe it!"

My eyes get big and I sit up straight.

There's a crowd that's cheering and going crazy.

Then a booming voice announces, "And in his first ever pro tour victory, BRRRROOOKLYYYYN WRIGHT!"

There's more cheering and then the announcer voice says, "Brooklyn, tell us how you're feeling!"

B's voice gets even louder, like he's using a microphone now. "I'd like to thank my dad, my sponsors, and the great fans here in Oahu that came out to support us, but I wouldn't even be here if it weren't for one special girl." His voice gets quieter, almost like he's speaking just to me. "Keats, you told me to follow my dreams wherever they took me and even though you're not here with me, know I wouldn't be here without you. I love you, Keats." Then he yells, "Here's to causing a little chaos!"

The crowd goes crazy and the call disconnects.

Oh my gosh. He did it!

He won!

Happy tears stream down my face.

Then it suddenly dawns on me that I'm not the only one who just heard what B said.

I see the hurt look on Aiden's face. I jump out of the hot tub quickly, saying, "Uh, I need a minute."

Then I run down to the beach and cry.

I cry for everything I'm missing out on.

And because Aiden just heard B say he loves me.

I cry for all the hurt I'm causing everyone.

Maybe I should just walk out into the ocean and never

come back.

DAMIAN PLOPS DOWN in the sand next to me. "I'm an idiot. I got excited and put it on speaker, not even thinking about Aiden. I hope I didn't screw things up for you."

"It's okay, Damian. I'm not mad."

"For what it's worth, I get it now. You're stuck. You can't go forward and you can't go back. You're like a hamster on a wheel, spinning and spinning but going nowhere."

I sniffle and wipe the haze of tears from my face. "Exactly."

"The last time we talked, when you told me you were cracked, I didn't get it. And other than the first night, I haven't seen it. You looked like your normal happy self. But the look on your face when you got out of the hot tub. You couldn't hide it. You looked exactly like you did at your dad's funeral. I'm so sorry I haven't been more understanding. There's no excuse for why I haven't talked to you more. Been more supportive. I was busy doing stuff that didn't matter."

He wraps his arm around me and pulls me toward his shoulder.

"Damian, I don't think you can understand what you haven't gone through. Now do you see why I'm not going back? This is killing me. If Vincent hadn't happened, I know I would've been there today. I would've celebrated with him in person. I'm so incredibly proud of him."

"But then you wouldn't have met Aiden. I like him. And I like his sister a whole lot."

"I like Aiden too. That's why when I left to come here, I wasn't planning on going back. I can't take heartbreak too. I can't form a lasting relationship with someone when I'm lying to him."

"I think Aiden loves you."

"Which only makes it worse. I don't want to hurt him. His nose got broken because of me. Imagine what Vincent could do to him. And what it will do to his heart when he finds out the truth."

"So you like B more?"

"Everything with B is familiar. I know what to expect from him. And he's growing up. He's not smoking. God, his eyes are so beautiful when he's not high. And what he did for Gracie. He's like home . . ."

"But?"

"But my idea of home is kinda starting to shift."

"Like how you said Aiden made your loft feel like home?"

"That's the real reason I can't go back there. Because Aiden ruined it."

"Keats, how? What did he do?"

I touch my mouth and start crying harder.

"He ruined it like he ruined my lips. When he was there, it felt like home. And I don't ever want to kiss another boy."

"Then don't."

"But I promised B."

"Why did you promise him?"

"Because I want to go home. I want my life back. I want to press rewind."

"If you did that, then where would Aiden be?"

"That's the problem. I don't know where all my friends from school would fit into my life. And I'm really worried about B now."

"Why?"

"Because if Vincent hears what B just said. It's gonna

put a big target on him."

"Do you still love him?"

"I've always loved him. It sounds bad that I dated Sander for so long and was in love with someone else, but I was. He was my dream guy."

"Even before you and B got together—those two years you were friends—everyone knew. Why do you think none of the other guys ever hit on you?"

"Because they thought of me as B's."

He nods his head.

"I even wrote a song about it. Because I wanted that. I wanted to find a girl who would look at me that way. I know you were fighting some when you were on tour with us, but I always believed you'd work it out. I thought you'd marry him someday."

A wedding flashes into my mind. Our beach at sunrise. Even though it's a crazy time to have guests, it would have to be at sunrise.

Stop it.

Don't do this to yourself, Keatyn.

Think about now.

"Can I be honest with you?" Damian asks.

"No, Damian, lie to me. I'm sick of the truth. I want you to tell me it's all going to be okay. Just lie to me."

I start crying again, so he hugs me tighter. Which, in turn, makes me cry harder as I remember the way he hugged me the night of my party.

I determinedly stop crying and state, "It was love at first sight for you and Peyton."

He looks at me funny and says, "Yeah, I told you that."

I pull out of his arms, get to my feet, and pull him up with me. "Come on. We have something important to do."

"Where are we going?"

I smile at him. "We're going to do what I should've done the second you met her. We're going to make a wish."

He smiles at me and starts to go down the pathway toward the mermaid fountain.

"No, this way." I lead him up to my room. "I have something more powerful."

"Did you make your wish when you got here?"

"I did."

"Did you wish the same thing you always do? That you will find your prince?"

"Yes. Then Aiden gave me his penny and told me to wish for something new."

"For him?"

"I think that's what he wanted me to wish for."

"But what did you wish for?" I hesitate, so he adds, "We decided a long time ago that it's legal to share your wish with your very best friend."

"I wished for my life back."

"That's a good wish. And it would solve all your problems at once."

"Not really, but it's the only wish that would *allow* me to solve them."

I look up and see Peyton standing on the veranda. Her cover-up is moving in the breeze as she looks out into the ocean. And it makes me feel good to know that I'm not giving up on the fairy tale. And if I can't have it, I'm going to make sure someone else gets it.

As we enter the turret and climb the stairs to my room, I say, "You know, when I was little I always thought I'd marry you."

"That's just cuz I have a castle on the beach."

"And you sing like a good frog."

I lead him into my closet, grab my suitcase, unzip the

top part of it, and pull out Tink.

Damian starts laughing. "You carry around a wand? Seriously?"

"Don't laugh. Avery selflessly gave me this Tinker Bell wand when I left home and told me I could make a wish on it. She was selfless and I'm selflessly using my wish for you— which makes it doubly powerful."

I grab his pinkie with mine, wave the wand at him, and wish, "*I wish Damian and Peyton will live happily ever after.*"

Damian grins at me, then runs his hand through his hair. "I can't believe I'm excited that you just made a wish for me on a plastic wand. Jesus, I'm in deep. It's just so amazingly weird, though, how we're both here, don't you think?" He stops in his tracks, pulls out his phone, and types something down.

I know that means he just thought of a song lyric he doesn't want to forget.

"I better go find Aiden and talk to him," I tell Damian.

We go downstairs and see Aiden pacing the beach, his footsteps kicking up sand.

"Keatyn, if you love him, don't let your circumstances get in the way."

"I don't want to hurt him."

"You can't have love without risking heartache, and he seems like he's more than willing to take the risk." I nod, but don't move, so he pushes me toward the beach. "It's time to go see if you and Aiden have enough dirt to survive that phone call."

I must not look convinced, because he adds, "And if you still want him to get on the plane without you tomorrow, I'll personally see to it."

FROM THE BEGINNING.
11PM

"HEY," I SAY, for lack of a better line.

"You've been crying," he says, sitting down next to me.

I nod. "I have lot of conflicting emotions."

"Did you tell me the truth about when you saw him at your sister's birthday party?"

"Yes."

He runs his hand through his hair and shakes his head. I realize now that I won't have to tell him goodbye tomorrow. That he's going to walk away gladly.

Hell, he'll probably thank me.

"I was just stalking him online. He doesn't seem to have a personal page, but he does have a fan type page that he made in August. The first three pictures he uploaded were of you. The two of you." Aiden lowers his head a little, his eyes shiny. "You looked happy with him."

"I was happy with him. Most of the time."

"Tell me about him. About the two of you. When we fought that day, you defended him."

I feel his pinkie grab ahold of mine. It's a simple gesture, but one that speaks volumes.

He's not running away this time.

"Of course I defended him. You were way off base thinking our relationship was about sex. Do you really want to hear all of this?"

"Yeah, I do. From the beginning. From when you met."

"My mom traveled for her job, so I was tutored. I never went to a real school."

"But wait, I thought you met Damian at school."

"Not a regular school. We shared the same tutor and depending on where his dad was and where my mom was, sometimes we ended up in class together. Anyway, I was around adults a lot. My mom always said that I was mature and worldly. But I was very naive about some things. Like relating to kids my age. I watched a lot of movies. Read a lot of books. And I had this fantasy school experience in my head."

Aiden squeezes my pinkie and laughs. "Let me guess, you planned it out down to the shoes."

I smile at him. "Kinda. So it was the summer of my fifteenth birthday. My mom had been with my stepdad for a while, and we were living on the beach. It was the first time since before my dad died that we had a real home, and I knew this was my chance to go to a real high school. I'd seen the movie *High School Musical* and wanted that. That perfect high school experience. I wanted to be the most popular girl, date the most popular guy, and if the basketball team had broken out into song during practice, I would have joined in."

Aiden touches my face. "You're so adorable."

I get tears in my eyes again. Because how could he even say that after what just transpired? He should hate me. "Why do you think that?"

"I can see the sparkle in your eyes. How excited you were. It's like you believed your life could be a fairy tale."

"Well, I used to."

"We'll get to that later. Keep going with your story."

"So, I got two things for my birthday. They told me I could go to a real high school and they got me a surfboard. My stepdad explained how to surf, then sent me out to do it. I spent hours in the water trying to get it right." I pause, because I can still see it so clearly in my mind. "And then *he* walked down the beach and helped teach me. Shaggy blond hair and the bluest eyes I'd ever seen. And it was like *bam*—I was in love. Fast forward two years. He'd become one of my best friends, and I was living out what I thought was my perfect high school experience. I was dating the hottest guy at school. And I was popular."

"That doesn't surprise me. You're in everything."

"I wasn't there. My friends considered school activities uncool. I only played soccer. But we had partying down to an art form."

"That surprises me. I just can't picture you a drunken mess."

"I wasn't. My perfect boyfriend was the mess."

"He's the guy you dated for a year and a half but didn't sleep with?"

"Yeah."

"So he *was* gay?"

I roll my eyes at him. "Yes, but I didn't know it at the time. So it's prom night. I had a beautiful, sexy dress, great shoes, and knew it was the night I'd finally lose my virginity."

Aiden tilts his head. "But he didn't want to because he was gay?"

"I still didn't know he was gay, but I guess. He dropped me off at my door after the party and barely kissed me."

Aiden laughs. Like he's really laughing. I'm afraid he's losing it.

"Why are you laughing about this? It's not really funny."

"Because our proms were like horrible mirror opposites."

"What do you mean?"

"You're going to laugh at my stupidity."

I run my fingers across the top of his hand. "No, I won't."

"I did what you wanted. Got a nice hotel room. Even had chocolate covered strawberries and champagne." He laughs again. "Honestly, I didn't come up with that. Shark helped me plan it. Said that's what girls want. What she'd want. I think he'd taken a poll or something."

"Who was your date?"

He gulps and looks at me intently. "It was Chelsea." He runs his hand through his hair again, like he's struggling to tell me.

I want to scream and throw a fit. But after what he just heard and how he's calmly talking to me about it, I can't. I bite both my lip and my tongue as he continues.

"I thought . . ." He shakes his head at himself. "Remember you asked me about my most embarrassing moment?"

"Yeah."

"We'd been hanging out since I asked her to Prom a few weeks earlier. We'd done everything but sex, so this was supposed to be the big night. I was going to tell her I loved her, ask her to be my girlfriend, and then we'd do it."

"Did you love her or did you just want sex?"

He shakes his head. "Honestly, probably a little of both. I liked her, but I wanted more. I should preface this by saying that I pretty much thought I was the shit. Up until that point, I had dated and slept with whoever I wanted. I wasn't like Logan, who was totally in love with Maggie. But after seeing them together, I wanted that. That one person to love me, not just who wanted to hook up with me."

"Okay."

"So, we're at the dance. It's a slow song. The lights are dim. And even though I had planned it out differently, it just felt right. So, I told her I loved her, then and there, and asked her to be my girlfriend."

"That's sweet, Aiden."

He rolls his eyes and sighs. "She was sort of drunk, and when I asked, she let out a scream and started laughing hysterically. Then she proceeded to grab two of her girlfriends and loudly tell them what just happened and how she couldn't believe I didn't know she was dating—and fucking—two other guys."

"And everyone heard?"

"Yeah."

I wrap my arms around Aiden in a hug. "That must've been awful. What'd you do then?"

"Well, it gets worse. Believe it or not, that wasn't the embarrassing part."

"What else happened?"

He looks at me tentatively. "I'm not sure if I should tell you this, but I need you to know. Especially after what happened with Chelsea. Because if you ever only heard just part of the story . . ."

I put both my hands on his face, forcing him to look at me. "It's okay, Aiden. You just had to listen to my ex tell me that he loves me."

"That was rough."

"I know it was. I'm sorry. Please tell me."

"So, Logan and Maggie—I swear, I totally ruined their night—anyway, they took me to an after party. We did some shots. Well, I did quite a few shots. And there were a couple of girls there who felt sorry for me."

My mind is trying to figure out why he wouldn't want to tell me this.

Wait. "A couple of girls?"

He hangs his head in embarrassment and nods. "Yes. Two. My life was out of control. Eastbrooke was a blur of drinking, girls, and sports. And although my friends were proud of me, I wasn't very proud of myself." He pauses and looks at me. "You haven't walked away yet."

"I've done some stupid things too, Aiden. Things I'm not really proud of. So then you just decided to change?"

"Sort of. I went back to my hotel room. By then, I had sobered up and was feeling pretty bad about myself. So I sat out on the balcony, drank the champagne alone—straight out of the bottle—and, as the sun was almost ready to come up, I made a wish on the moon."

"You what?!"

"Silly, right? You're supposed to wish on shooting stars. But I was tipsy, couldn't find any, and the moon was just there."

"What did you wish for?" I say slowly in an almost reverent whisper.

"My perfect girl," he says wistfully, looking out at the moon shimmering above the ocean.

I feel like I just got punched in the gut.

Could he have really wished for me?

Could it be true?

"Um, Aiden, when was your Prom?"

"It was May thirteenth. Friday the thirteenth. Weird, huh? Having Prom on Friday the thirteenth like some bad horror movie. But I guess that was the only time they could get the venue. Probably because no one else wanted it then."

Aiden is speaking. Going on and on about Friday the thirteenth, but my mind is busy calculating. It was 2:30 when I got in my room the night I made my wish. A three hour time difference would be around 5:30am. Before the sun came up.

Oh. My. God.

"So after that, I didn't date anyone. Didn't do anything with anyone. Until you kicked a soccer ball at my head."

I start to cry.

I can't help it.

Fate is so, so cruel.

I want to tell him that I wished on the moon too. That he's my perfect boy.

But I can't tell him that.

Not when I have to tell him goodbye.

I have to make him believe I'm not it.

That it's someone else and that she's still out there waiting for him.

And that's when I lose it.

I put my face in my hands and start bawling.

Aiden puts his arm around my back. "Why are you crying so hard? Do you hate me? I'm so sorry. I should've told you before, but we were . . . And then everything . . . Please stop crying and tell me what you're thinking."

I look up at him and say the last thing in the world that I want to say to him. "Because I'm probably not the girl you wished for, Aiden."

He squints his eyes at me and shakes his head. "Is that because after what I told you, you don't want to be that girl?"

"No, it's not because of that."

"Then what is it?"

"I just don't think . . ."

He grabs my hand and places my palm on his chest. "Close your eyes. What do you feel?"

I close my eyes, only because it will be easier to finish this without looking at him. "I feel you breathing."

"Try again," he says in that voice. The voice that has the power to make me comply.

"I feel your heartbeat."

"No, what you feel is my heart beating for you. Always.

Only. Ever. For you."

I open my eyes and look at him, shaking my head. "How can you even say that? After everything?"

"Because I can feel it. And I know you feel it too."

"Love at first sight is just a crazy notion made up by hopeless romantics."

"There's a lot about us that's crazy, but there's a lot about us that's right. You belong with me, Boots."

"Because I couldn't be anyone else's?" I say before I think better of it.

I get the blazing love god smile. "So you do listen to what I say?"

I let out a little chuckle. "Maybe."

"I always thought Dawson was the reason you were holding back emotionally, but it was him, wasn't it?"

I nod.

He flips both our wrists over, exposing our fresh tattoos. "Did you know that each leaf on a four-leaf clover has a special meaning?"

I shake my head and let out a big sigh, trying to stop myself from crying.

"The first petal is for faith. You need to have faith in us. The second is for hope. The hope that we can get through whatever life throws at us. The third is for love. And the fourth is for luck. We already know that we're lucky together."

I notice that he skipped commenting on the love petal.

But then he grabs my hands and looks into my soul. "Look, this isn't at all how I wanted to do this. But I love you. A deep-within-my-soul, heartbreakingly beautiful kind of love."

I open my mouth to speak, but he holds up his hand. "No. I don't want you to say anything. And I'm not even saying *I love you* yet. When I say that, I want it to be perfectly right. Like out of one of your fairy tales. But I need you to know how I feel."

I wipe my tears and nod.

And then we kiss.

And this kiss kills me.

A knife straight through my heart kills me.

Because I feel that way too.

"You're still crying," he says, wiping away my tears.

"I know. I'm sorry."

"It's okay, baby. It's been a rough night. Let's go to bed."

Then he takes my hand, leads me to my turret, takes my dress off, puts his blue linen shirt on me, pulls me into bed, kisses me sweetly, and holds me tight.

Pretty soon, I notice that he's breathing heavily; asleep.

I glance at the clock, counting down the time I have left with him and holding him tighter than I ever have before.

SORTA LIKE FATE.
3AM

I CAN'T SLEEP. My brain is still counting down—ticking and ticking—the hours and, now, the minutes until I have to say goodbye.

My stomach hurts. My heart aches. I feel sick.

I still can't believe he wished on the moon.

But, yet, I know it's true. Deep down inside me, I know it's true.

And I don't want to leave him.

But I know I have to.

I know it's the only way.

I stare at him sleeping next to me.

Knowing it will be the last time.

I close my eyes and try to soak him in. The feel of his body curled into mine. His strong hand protectively holding my leg. The smell of his neck. The pace of his beating heart.

As I start to cry, I hear music. The same chords gently strummed across a guitar over and over. A soft, dreamy voice.

I slide out of bed, being careful not to wake Aiden, peek out the window, and see Damian sitting down by the water with his guitar.

I throw a robe around me and tiptoe out of the room.

"THAT'S PRETTY," I say, sitting down next to him. "Is it new?"

When he replies, I see the boy I used to know, who was a little unsure of his talent, not the confident man he's become. "I'm working on a song for her. I feel like I know everything about her but yet I don't know the most important thing."

"What's that?"

"How to make her mine. She's gorgeous. Sweet. My dream girl. When I walked up the beach, I felt like . . . I don't even know; it's hard to put into words. That's why I'm having a hard time with this song."

He studies me closely. "Are you and Aiden okay?"

I shrug, not knowing what to say.

"He had a chat with me. Like the talk Tommy had with me the night before I took you parking."

"We didn't go parking."

"You and I know why you wanted to go up there."

"Research for a role."

"Exactly. But Tommy didn't believe that. He basically told me if I touched you, he'd fuck me up."

"He wouldn't say that!"

"He didn't say that, but that was the message. Trust me."

"He's really protective of her. They've been through a lot together."

"I know about everything."

"Like what?"

"She told me all of it. Listed every reason why I shouldn't like her. What happened with her mom. Why she ended up at school. Why Aiden went there. Her affair with the teacher. Her friend threatening her. Her partying, activities, and the names and addresses of every boy she ever kissed."

"Why would you need their addresses?"

"So I can write each one a thank you note for being a dick to her."

"You really have been talking."

He nods. "And I told her everything about me. My past, the tour, and even the groupies. Now if I could just put in words how I felt when I first met her."

I think about how Aiden made me feel when I first met him. "Did you feel like she spoke to your soul? Or like she was a magnet that you couldn't help but be pulled toward?"

"That's exactly what it felt like. Hang on," he says as he writes the words *magnetic* and *soul* into the notes app on his phone. "She probably thinks I'm a freak because I can't stop staring at her, but I feel like I'm looking at my future. And that smile." He stops again and adds *smile* and *future* to his list.

"Wanna hear a funny story?"

He nods at me.

"I tutor Aiden in French. And one of the very first times we were in the library studying, he told me we were fate. That it was fate that we were there. That we both ended up at the same school. And I laughed at him . . ."

Damian starts typing, so I stop talking. "No, keep going," he says.

"Anyway, he asked me what the French word for fate was and it's . . ."

"*Sort*," Damian says slowly.

"Right. And then he said that we're sorta like fate."

He puts his palm into the air. "Hang on." He types some more then says, "What else?"

"Then he told me that he's going to ask me to marry him at the . . ." Tears start streaming down my face. Damian looks up from his phone.

"Marry you?"

"Yeah, at the top of the Eiffel Tower, at sunset."

"It sounds like something you would've scripted."

"It is better than anything I've ever scripted," I reply, hugging myself and trying not to have a total crying breakdown.

"Don't cry," he says, lightly punching my thigh. "Close your eyes and listen to this." He starts singing, *"You're my faith and inspiration. You're the ink in my tattoo. You're the water in my desert. All I can think about is you. You're the sun in all my sunsets. You're the wind in every breeze. You're the moon on my horizon. You're the one that makes me breathe."*

"That's beautiful, Damian."

"I need a chorus. Something about fate. And us being here. I'm gonna record us. Listen again and then sing the first thing that pops in your head. Okay. Here goes. *You're my faith and inspiration. You're the ink in my tattoo. You're the water in my desert. All I can think about is you. You're the sun in all my sunsets. You're the wind in every breeze. You're the moon on my horizon. You're the one that makes me breathe."*

I feel his words resonate in my heart and when he finishes, I sing, *"It's sorta like fate that we're together. It's sorta like fate that we're both here."*

He continues, *"It's sorta like you and me forever."*

"My destiny is clear."

"Holy shit. That's it," Damian says. "That's exactly it. You're a genius."

I give him a smile, then bite my lip so I won't start crying again.

Damian turns off the recorder and puts his hand on top of mine. "You still planning on telling him goodbye?"

"Yeah."

"Keats, I think that might be a mistake."

"You know I don't have a choice."

"Are you sure about that? I mean, have you really thought it all through?"

"Yes, there's no other way."

"What if I help you find another way? No one knows I'm here. If I went back with you, I could help."

I shake my head. "If you go back with her, I can't go back. And you can't help me."

"So, you're going to make me choose?"

"Yeah, Damian, I am. And your choice should be easy. If you love her like I think you do, don't you dare let her go."

"I love you too, you know."

"I know, but it's not the same." My eyes fill with tears. "Damian, will you promise me something?"

"Okay," he says tentatively.

"That didn't sound like a promise. I'm completely

serious about this. I *need* you to promise that you'll do this for me."

"Okay, I promise. What do you want me to do?"

"If I don't make it through this battle with Vincent. If I die. I need you to tell Aiden that I loved him."

Damian's eyes get huge and he lunges toward me, knocking his guitar into the sand. He grabs both my arms and says sternly, "Don't say that. Don't you dare say that."

"Just promise me, please. I can't do this if you don't promise."

He lets me go, looks into my eyes, and nods. "I promise, Keats."

"Thanks. I'm gonna go back to my room. Try to get a little sleep before—well, just before . . ."

Sunday, November 27th
I WISH NONE OF US HAD TO LEAVE.
6AM

I DOZED OFF at some point, but the clock is still ticking in my brain and I can't lie here any longer.

I wander down to the beach and find Damian still out in the cabana, asleep.

I go up to the house and grab a few of Inga's homemade oatmeal cookies and two cups of coffee and carry them out to the sand and wake him up.

"Shit," he says. "I can't believe I fell asleep out here."

I look out at the sky brightening as the sun rises behind us. "I didn't tell you, but something happened last night."

"Besides the call from Brook?"

"Yeah. I saw the green flash."

"You always say that."

"No, for real. We both saw it."

"You're totally in love with him."

"Yeah, pretty much."

"So why would you even *want* to give B a chance?"

"Because I promised."

"But why did you do that?"

"Because, Damian, he's the boy I've always dreamed about."

"And now, if they were both standing in front of you and you had to choose, who would you pick?"

"I had a dream like that. You were in it, but you were a wolf. We were all humans trapped in wolves bodies and I had to choose between the Brooklyn wolf and Aiden wolf. And I think you helped me somehow, because when I kissed one of them, I chose right. It was true love's kiss, it broke the curse, and all the wolves turned back into men."

"But you don't know who you kissed?"

"No."

"So what does that tell you?"

"I don't know."

"I do," he says confidently. "It tells you that you choose right. When the time is right, you'll choose the right one. Maybe that's the momentous decision you'll have to make. But still, I think you're making a mistake right now. I think you should be looking forward, not looking back."

"I am looking forward. I have to get my life back."

"I think you should go back to school."

"If I do that, you can't date Peyton."

"This sucks," he says, running his hands down the sides of his face. "So you're really going to do it? You're going to put him on the plane and say goodbye?"

"I have to, Damian."

"So where are you going?"

"I'm going to stay here for a few more days, if that's okay. I'll spend some time online looking at farm properties that I can lease quickly. I had originally thought I'd go somewhere in the Midwest, but now I'm leaning toward Texas. Did you know that in Texas if someone comes on your property, like trespasses, you can legally shoot them.

Well, at least I think so. I need to look and see if it's an actual law or if it's just Grandpa's bullshitting, but I do know they are a very gun-friendly state."

"So your plan is to learn how to shoot, then lure Vincent to Texas, where you will then shoot him for trespassing and it will be over?"

"Oh, I never thought of that. That's a really good idea. And one that wouldn't require the mob or jail time."

"Do you have other ideas?"

"I have a whole lot of ideas. One of which is just walking into Vincent's office and telling him I want to audition for his movie. See what happens."

"Keatyn, fuck! No way you can do that!"

"I love you, Damian, you know that. But, in this, only I have a say about what I can or can't do. When I saw Vincent in Vancouver, I wasn't so much scared as I was pissed."

"You weren't scared?"

I roll my eyes at him. "Fine. I was scared. Really scared. But I was really mad too. And the mad is starting to take over."

"You're mad because you want to be with Aiden."

"My life is unsettled because of Vincent. I'm mad because I can't see my family. I'm mad because my mom is freaking out scared. She's losing weight. Won't ride anywhere with Tommy. Thinks Vincent is going to kill them both. My own family was afraid of me. They were afraid I brought Vincent to them."

"But you would never do that."

"But, yet, I almost did. He was headed there. He had men on the plane with him. Men who looked like Garrett."

"Garrett scares me a little."

"He's been really nice to me. But tough, you know. And I love Cooper."

"He's the bodyguard?"

"Yeah, he's a badass. And it's really sad. His older sister was killed by a stalker—in fact it happened at Thanksgiving time."

Damian looks like he just got the wind knocked out of him.

"I would seriously die if anything happened to you. You always have been and always will be my best friend."

"I thought about faking my death. Even about killing myself."

Damian's eyes get huge and he grabs my shoulders and shakes me. "Tell me that is *not* part of your plan."

"It's not. I don't think it's just about me anymore. James said something about Vincent wanting both me and Mom. I'm positive there's stuff going on that they aren't telling me. So my being gone wouldn't solve my family's problems."

Unless I take Vincent down with me, I think, but don't dare say that out loud.

"This is all just crazy."

"Yeah, it is."

He gives me a hug and says, "I'm gonna go shower before Peyton wakes up. There's a lot I need to tell her. And you need to talk to Aiden. When are you going to tell him?"

"Right before you leave for the airport. I'll tell him and just not go with."

"You think he's going to accept that?"

"That's the other thing I need you to do, Damian. Make sure he gets on that plane and goes home."

I MOVE FROM the cabana to go sit in the sand. I close my eyes, sit still, and just breathe.

I need to say something to Peyton about not going back

too.

But I can't come up with anything.

The truth is, I don't want her to go back to Eastbrooke without me. I don't want to miss dancing during basketball season, or our competition, or the first big snowstorm, or Winter Formal, or French weekend . . .

"Hey," Peyton says, sitting down beside me. "You're up early."

"Yeah."

"I can't believe it's already time to leave. Have you seen Damian this morning?"

"Yeah, he went to shower a little bit ago."

"He says he's writing me a song."

"He is. He was working on it last night on the beach after you went to sleep."

"We slept together," she whispers. "And he wasn't there this morning."

"That doesn't mean what you think it does. Damian is creative and driven and when he's inspired, he has to get it out of him."

"So does he write every girl a song? Is that, like, his thing?" She sighs.

I think to when I asked Aiden if he brought every girl lunch, or clovers, or cake.

"No, it's not his thing. He's never written a love song before."

"Sure he has." She quotes, "*Her eyes get bright every time he's around. The ocean waves beat out her heart's sound. Their love begins as a ripple and grows into a tidal wave. But he'd surf through uncertainty just to see that gaze. Oh baby, if you only knew, Oh, baby, the feelings I have for you, Oh baby, if you could only see, Oh, baby, it needs to be you and me.* He's totally got a crush on someone. Or has a girlfriend. Or something."

"One, I would've told you if he had a girlfriend. And two, that song is about me."

"He's in love with you?"

"No, silly. It's about me and the surfer guy. We were friends for a couple years before we got together and supposedly everyone could see we were in love."

"What about *forget about him, come surf the crowd with me, it ain't the water, but baby it's plain to see*—" She stops. "That song really resonates with me. About how she's popular but no one sees that she cries herself to sleep."

"Remember I told you on the plane about how I became the biggest bitch ever?"

"Yeah . . . So that song's about you too?"

"Inspired by what happened, yes."

"Does he have a secret crush on you?"

"Damian is like my brother. Absolutely no crushing. Well, except for the big one he has on you."

She gives me a blazing smile. "Do you think so?"

"I know so."

"He says he wants to see me again. That this isn't just a vacation hookup and that it's the start of an epic romance."

"He's not like other guys, Peyton. He's honest and he doesn't play games. He's the kind of guy you can trust. And now that he's back in the states, he'll probably be all over the internet, so you can keep an eye on him."

"I'm not going to stalk him."

"Annie says it's not stalking, it's research. Nothing wrong with that," I tease. "So, are you all packed?"

"Yeah, but I don't want to leave here," she says quietly.

I see Aiden walking toward us and say, "I wish none of us had to leave."

"I'm all packed," he says, sitting down next to us.

Peyton's phone dings. "Oh, I have to go," she says and then rushes off toward Damian's room.

Aiden seems lost in thought. He keeps tilting his head like he wants to ask me a question but doesn't know if he should.

"What?" I finally say.

"Can I ask you a question about your ex?"

"Uh, sure."

"If he loves you, why aren't you together? Why doesn't he come see you at school? Why aren't you at his competitions? Like, this weekend. You were off school. Why didn't you go watch?"

"Uh, well, because I'm not allowed to see him."

"But yet you have. You saw him on Labor Day break before you went to the Hamptons. And then again when you went to the birthday party."

"Yeah, but we weren't supposed to see each other."

"Do your parents not like him?"

"No, my family likes him. It's complicated, Aiden."

"I'm sure it is, but I need to understand."

"Maybe it isn't my parents who don't want us to see each other."

"So, his parents?"

"His dad." I don't want to flat out lie to Aiden, but B's dad did play a big role in his leaving the way he planned to, even before Vincent happened. He was afraid I'd hold him back.

"But you said he's older than you. Why would he even have to listen to his dad?"

"Because even though his dad lined him up with some sponsors, he still needed his financial support to do it. He has a trust fund, but he doesn't get it until he's, like, thirty or something. The deal was that he'd try it for a year and see if he was good enough. And if he turned out to be good enough, he'd probably get full sponsorship, and then could do whatever he wanted."

"So, after a year, he's coming home? To you?"

"In theory, yes," I say, because that was the original plan. Sort of.

"When's that year up?"

"On my birthday. August."

He reaches out and grabs both of my hands in his. "I'll take it."

"What do you mean?"

"Boots, I may not be out winning tournaments for you, but I'm with you every day. I'd much rather have that. And if in August you wanna go see him, then go. I'm up for the competition. By then, we'll have built such a strong foundation that no one could tear it down. So your choice will be easy." He gives me an adorably cocky smile and points to himself. "Me. Speaking of that, why haven't you packed yet? Don't we have to leave for the airport soon?"

Oh gosh. This is it. This is where I finally have to do it.

I've been dreading this moment since we stepped off the plane.

"Yes, you do have to leave for the airport soon."

"What do you mean, *you*? And why do you look sad again?"

"Because I'm not going with you. I'm not going back to Eastbrooke."

"Why not?"

"Family stuff, kinda."

"Then why did you let me come with you? Give me hope? Why didn't you kick me off the plane?"

"Because I didn't handle it well when we were at school. Things felt unsettled, and I wanted to give you closure. Give us closure. I didn't do it to hurt you, Aiden. I just wanted to be able to say goodbye."

Aiden stands up quickly and paces in the sand in front of me. "Where are you going?"

"Probably France," I say, pushing back tears.

Aiden pulls me off the sand and into his arms. The wind blows my hair across my face in front of me. Aiden pushes it behind my ear, gets close to me, and says softly, "Then I'm moving to France too."

"You're what?"

"Wherever you go, I go."

"What? No. What about your sister?"

He looks over my shoulder, so I glance behind me to see Peyton happily laughing and swinging her feet off the edge of the pool, Damian sitting next to her.

"I think it's time I start living my life for me," he says.

"But, Aiden, it's not that easy. You have school."

"School is overrated. Let's stay here."

"But—"

He kisses me, effectively stopping me from speaking.

When the kiss ends, he gently pulls away and looks at me seriously. His eyes tell me everything I already know. "Keatyn, I mean it. Wherever you go, I go. I don't have a choice."

"Sure you do—"

He pulls my hand up and places it on his chest.

"You have my heart and I kinda need it to survive."

"But—"

He kisses me again. A good, long, powerful tongue kiss. Either I'm becoming weaker or he's definitely becoming more powerful.

"Do you trust me?" he says, still holding my hand against his chest.

"Yes."

"Good. Because when I said we're going to be together forever, I meant it."

Tears run down my face because this is exactly what I dreamed a boy would say to me.

But my life isn't a dream.

He sweeps my hair behind my neck and kisses it.

He must think he needs to infuse me with more love potion.

But I never really needed it.

He's had a piece of my heart since the moment I laid eyes on him.

"Forever is a really, really long time, Aiden," I say softly.

"And I was thinking just the opposite, Boots. Forever isn't going to be nearly long enough for us."

The End

About the Author

Jillian Dodd® is a USA Today and Amazon Top 10 best-selling author. She writes fun binge-able romance series with characters her readers fall in love with—from the boy next door in the That Boy series to the daughter of a famous actress in The Keatyn Chronicles® to a spy who might save the world in the Spy Girl® series. Her newest series include London Prep, a prep school series about a drama filled three-week exchange, and the Sex in the City-ish chick lit series, Kitty Valentine.

Jillian is married to her college sweetheart, adores writing big fat happily ever afters, wears a lot of pink, buys way too many shoes, loves to travel, and is distracted by anything covered in glitter.

58230865R00104